EX LIBRIS

VINTAGE **CLASSICS**

ROSEMARY TONKS

Rosemary Tonks (1928–2014) was a colourful figure in the London literary scene during the 1960s. She published two poetry collections, *Notes on Cafés and Bedrooms* and *Iliad of Broken Sentences*, and six novels, from *Opium Fogs* to *The Halt During the Chase*. Tonks wrote for the *Observer*, *The Times*, *New York Review of Books*, *Listener*, *New Statesman* and *Encounter*, and presented poetry programmes for the BBC.

ALSO BY ROSEMARY TONKS

The Bloater

Businessmen as Lovers

The Halt During the Chase

ROSEMARY TONKS

The Way Out of Berkeley Square

VINTAGE CLASSICS

1 3 5 7 9 10 8 6 4 2

Vintage Classics is part of the Penguin Random House group of companies
whose addresses can be found at global.penguinrandomhouse.com

First published in Great Britain by The Bodley Head in 1970
This paperback first published in Vintage Classics in 2024

penguin.co.uk/vintage-classics

A CIP catalogue record for this book is available from the British Library

ISBN 9781784879310

Typeset in 10.57/15pt Stempel Garamond LT Std
by Jouve (UK), Milton Keynes
Printed and bound in Great Britain by Clays Ltd, Elcograf S.p.A.

The authorised representative in the EEA is Penguin Random House Ireland,
Morrison Chambers, 32 Nassau Street, Dublin D02 YH68

Penguin Random House is committed to a sustainable future
for our business, our readers and our planet. This book is made
from Forest Stewardship Council® certified paper.

To the Beach Luxury Hotel, the De Luxe Hotel, and the Bristol Hotel, Karachi; to Johnny; and above all to Micky.

1

'I'm thirty, and I'm stuck.'

This thought comes to me the moment I get into bed at half-past eleven, and wakes me up again at about five o'clock the next morning. At five o'clock it increases the heart-beat so that the whole body is alerted by the thudding; and a young woman's body lying wide awake, shuddering, alone in bed at such a time has only one other refrain: 'I'm being wasted.' You can stretch your limbs with all the unnecessary strength of a young cat, or you can make a circle of your backbone knowing that it's as fine and rippling as an eel's, but you are playing for nobody and if you put out your hand and feel about in the bed, it's empty. And that makes you lie still again. 'Better to be alone than with the wrong person.' Is it? I remember Michael, my brother, saying to me: 'There are nights when I'd . . . go to bed with a frog!'

Michael's in Karachi. I had a letter today. It's on the little pink velvet chair with the buttoned back, the one beside my bed. There's a heap of books squashed against it; they're all ready to fall. Each book sticks out at a different angle. Does this mean I have a disorderly mind? If these were my father's books, they would be built up tightly like a pillar of salt. No: on second thoughts, my father only takes one book to bed with him, reads about five pages, stops in the middle of a sentence, tidily sets the edge of the jacket into the pages, and then lays it across the bedside table with his good, big hand, perhaps the kindest, cleverest hand in the whole of London. I've had that hand on my head to reassure me when I've been anxious about something so many times. He tells me my head is not large enough. When he rests his gloved hand on my shoulder it's unaccountably heavy, really heavy, like a small leather dog, and seems to push me down – suppose we're standing out in the street, saying goodbye to friends – I feel that I must struggle to throw off the weight of it. And when I wriggle it gives him an opportunity to smile at me, and at the same time to reproach me. 'Rejecting my hand?' That's what his face says openly. And yet there's guile in it. I'm involved again in a test, which I've failed, and which he made sure I would fail by laying upon my shoulder a hand over-heavy with love, with control, guidance, and financial security. So I bow my head, overcome by love. And the hand rests there with intolerable pressure.

I can hear my father going to bed just down the passage. The doors of the cupboards in his dressing-room close on roller-bolt springs; they go bump-bump-bump every night, rather like well-bred dodgem cars. In one cupboard there's a shelf loaded with yellow and green eau-de-colognes; coloured and white handkerchiefs of different qualities are piled up here, with neater corners than my books. If you unscrew one of the bottles of eau-de-cologne and sniff the wet wine-glass inside, you enter a refreshing continental world where light-hearted people are always clinking cut-glass and spending the lire or franc notes which line the rest of the shelf. There are also numbers of middle-aged Yale keys, as though to secret apartments all over the world. And yet I know my father's life and habits intimately, and he is simplicity itself. He loves a good home. That's why I'm still here. To keep house for him. (The house is in Holland Park.) His happiness lies in a well-organised domestic life; windows that are polished, spoons and forks whose silver is white-shiny; if you put out a fork with that tarnished rainbow on the prongs his eye picks on it like a falcon's, and he can't swallow his meat. We have a mouse living somewhere in the house, and you can always read his domestic humour by the way he refers to it. When things are going well in his business, this mouse is just a little field-mouse, a wholesome animal which has strayed in, possibly a harmless little female. But on bad days, it's 'a damn great rat', a male rodent to be hunted down and exterminated by me, or I shall get the sack. I've begun to wonder more and more about this; if I don't give good service, will I, in fact, be given the sack? I think it's dangerous to housekeep for your father, because in a sense you are marrying him. When my mother died, he was lost and begged and begged me to stay with him. And I stayed. Gradually we all three got over her death. Michael was the first to get restless. He was sent down from Oxford, and then they had rows every single day. Finally he got a room and left. The last thing he said to my father was:

'If you want to know what's driving me out, it's the gluey pots in the kitchen.'

I can see my father now, standing in the middle of the

sitting-room, taking this in; at fifty-five the picture of an elegant, middle-aged man. He's nearly bald but very handsome with curved black eyebrows. It happens that he is extremely fond of good soup, and likes to make it himself in old aluminium saucepans which have had a battering so that the lids don't fit tightly and the essence leaks out and somehow gets upstairs without being noticed and reasserts itself strongly in Michael's bedroom curtains. My father didn't know about this; his study, his dressing-room, his bedroom, all smell of herbal furniture cream. And he himself is always so perfectly bathed and dressed, with psychedelic zig-zags in his ties and handkerchiefs nowadays, and narrow supple ankles with velvet-fine socks . . . so far away from the idea of a gluey pot that he staggered a little when Michael said it, as though he'd received it full in the face. And I remember he even looked down at his waistcoat as though the words had lodged there as well and could easily be scrubbed off with Beaucaire if only it was done straight away.

Bump. That's the last cupboard. Now he'll re-enter his bathroom and run a glass of water to take to bed with him. Ah; he's going to gargle. A low mumbling sound, healthy, aquatic, like the sea in the Blue Grotto. He blows his nose quickly and thriftily. There's a pause, and then the sharp snapping of the brass electric light switch . . . so it must be nearly eleven-twenty. His tread, when he goes along the passage to his bedroom, is a curious loping movement, due partly to the slippers, but also I think to the fact that he wants to leave behind his orderly, calculating personality in his dressing-room and take on the boyishness, the naturalness which he associates with all the good sleep he had in his youth. And so the last thing I hear is this curious young and hopeful pattering, there's carelessness in it, something which is normally almost outside the range of my father's personality.

Now he's closed his door and I'm alone. I'll just re-read Michael's letter before going to sleep with my thirty-year-old thoughts. I loll my hand out for it . . . how frail rice-paper is.

I read a paragraph, and realise he isn't really unhappy. I suppose that's because he's only twenty. His likes and dislikes haven't hardened off. He says Karachi is the dust capital of the East; but in the middle of the bazaar is an excellent bookshop selling Joyce, Hazlitt and Stephen Crane. He can't write a line because of the din which continues for twenty-four hours a day, but he is moving out to the desert where he is to live in the upper part of a new concrete house which has just been put up miles away from anywhere. No one else will take this flat because it's so isolated; consequently it's cheap, and the concrete's grey paste has only just dried out. He's mad with joy at the thought of the peace out there. The desert is a flat, rubble desert and the Indus river gets lost in the dry, cracked plain before reaching the sea. Michael writes that he does everything that is dangerous; walks without shoes on, drinks unboiled milk, swims out into the Indian Ocean as far as the sharks are said to come in. He went to a doctor on account of certain sores on his head and was told: 'You're the brownest white skin I've seen in Karachi.' But those sores on the head? He says it's nothing; he's had his head shaved. And his new hair prickles and is growing out in tight curls, nearly white. Oh Michael! You'll be a beauty then! Everything to excess, in that green, narrow, muscular body. Father always behaved as though all the wildness of the family had been bred into Michael. They disapprove of one another. All Michael says about him is: 'Are you still keeping his purple socks clean?' but then he immediately goes on: 'The literary sensibility here is OK. There are certain people who know a good deal. Can you believe it, after London?' He says the bazaar smells of incense, burnt soap, and fireworks, and that high and low roll themselves in silk like bales of cloth, and get lost there and sleep themselves back to life. Michael never gets lost. He says that since he came to the East his eyes have quite literally increased in size. He also says that when lepers ask him for baksheesh he *has* to touch their hands when he gives them money . . . 'due entirely to reading the stupid Christians' Bible. Why can't I drop it in their bowls?'

Holding sheets of paper outside the bedclothes makes your hands very cold, exactly as though you are holding them out of a window. Michael's hands, fresh from that street-touching, folded up these sheets and now my London hands, pale and smooth and cold, hold the same paper. I'm not exactly afraid for him, but I'm wary. There's too much excitement and daring in the letter. Is it any good writing back: 'Be careful'? I doubt it. He could be here, in this warm city bedroom with its rosewood chest of drawers and dressing table – with earrings on it, long flashing ones of teardrop glass from Czechoslovakia, which need the chip repaired – if he *wanted*. He could be sitting here, on my bed, talking to me with all the sweetness (Father would call it wildness) of a totally innocent human being, saying:

'You look dazzling in those earrings, silly. Let's go to Annabel's and break them in.'

But if we went to Annabel's, it would be paid for by my father. And so we wouldn't go. Because Michael can't bear *that*.

I always think I can change and improve life for Michael, and I've promised to do this in so many words. But at the moment all I'm able to do is to steal pieces off the plate of this life with my father, and give them to him. I write to him nearly every day to give him emotional security. But to make such a large promise, the promise of a life, to an innocent person is a serious matter. He trusts me and believes in me. His job in life is to write masterpieces; poems. In order to do this he keeps his body and his mind in very good order. He has so many physical skills; especially swimming. He says his diction in poetry must come from life, without obstacles, and therefore he must begin, at the very least, by being good at life, better than the others. His body has to be, and is, perfect. Just as his judgment has to be better than the judgment of others in the war of ideas. Michael says everything you are going to do you do straight away, before you're ready. He says we have only one real emotional responsibility to one another, and that is that we must *never break down*. He's supposed to be writing a biography of an Indian mystic, for which he's had an advance of money. But he had the idea of selling commercial television in Karachi as well, in order to be able to buy the books he can't afford in London – 'Oh Pigeon, to see an idiot carrying glossy books!'

But having made that promise to him, I'm finding out that although you can organise someone's environment to make it pleasing, you can't organise the heaped-up furniture in their minds, which is where the life comes from. You can't force them to be happy if their way of being happy is to be half-unhappy.

It's a relief that he's away, because I can't be myself when I'm spending so many thoughts on him. Father's bad enough, he takes my time in physical terms. But with Michael out of the country I've begun to take stock of myself, and to want things again. The other day I was entertaining a party for my father and we'd taken three very lumpy couples to the Savoy, where I was sitting (controlled and graceful) by the floor, when I suddenly sniffed the razzmataz music, the sorbet on my plate, and the atmosphere, and decided I liked it and needed it. But not on these terms. Father whispered: 'You're looking awfully grim. Couldn't you smile a bit? It makes it so difficult for me.' At that exact moment a voice inside me was screaming: 'Nightclubs! Ultraviolet light! Deafening music! Stupidity, and smooth, bad behaviour!' I just scrunched up my napkin as though I'd taken a huge decision, and then tamely laid it on the table in the dark, and spread my fingers out over it (as if to keep it quiet) in the way I spread them when I search about in my empty bed for another drowsy body. Not the body of my father sleeping down the passage, or of my brother either.

I'd better put the light out. I have to roll over because it's across on the other side of the bed; the button is faulty so it flashes a few times for good measure. Then darkness.

The moment it's dark I can see Michael touching lepers in Karachi.

I hate being made to suffer for him at a distance like

this! In a moment, I'm extremely angry with him. I have to roll towards the lamp again, switch it on, and write down something to go into my letter to him tomorrow. I write: 'Why on earth do you have to go around fingering lepers? It's so phoney. They must hate it, and wonder what on earth you're doing. I would.'

He'll be so angry. The insult's perfect. I'm very pleased, switch out the lamp again and go to sleep laughing.

There are five manila folders with bills and correspondence in them on the sitting-room table. I'm checking for my father the specification of a property conversion he's taken up. It's a pretty little town house in Chelsea. He's given it to me to run to 'keep me out of mischief'; if it goes well I'm to get a commission. 'And you'll learn how to do up a house, and furnish it correctly. Invaluable experience.' I suppose it is, but for *me*? I now know where I can expect to find every single sort of door handle and escutcheon. I study the wattage necessary to light difficult rooms. I know that kitchen units must be ordered nine months in advance; and in the draughty empty house I crawled on the floors measuring dusty, coarse boards. Every bill must be kept for tax purposes; most of the cheap invoices (they're as transparent as one of Michael's letters) seem to be orange (the colour of all bachelors' lampshades) or blue. This rather nice ice-cream pink if a final notice from the London Electricity Board; I write 'paid' on it and hide it well down in the folder; Father hates that sort of trivial inefficiency. I always find it difficult to lift the essential information from such bills, the date, and the amount you actually have to pay. It's like trying to find out which day of the week it is in the *Radio Times* – if it's a ten-minute programme, it's over by the time you've got there. How important this cheque-book of Father's is, thick and springy like a minute steak. I fill it in, and put my counter-signature below where his will go. This signature has nothing to do with my normal hand. I invented it when Father opened my account, and it's a matter of self-esteem that I do it exceptionally fast – illegible lightning. It's the only way I can feel myself the equal of anything as valuable as a cheque-book, where every page has the look of a banknote in its own right.

It occurs to me that I'm perfectly happy. Sitting at home, doing accounts, with a grey wishy-washy afternoon going by outside! Am I going to be able to live the simple life after all? Empty, intelligent afternoons, meals on the dot, duties, checking the laundry, going shopping correctly dressed, country house parties correctly dressed, an occasional ball (correctly dressed), and different brands of conversation to go with each, but always calm, cheerful, lightweight, harmonious, reasonable. Then I suddenly hear Michael saying: 'I opened the book fully intending to read it, when I saw the words "much vaunted". And I had to close it again.' Ah, that's it. I always think I can go through with ordinary life, until someone says 'much vaunted', *mea culpa* or, an even better one, 'bruited abroad' and then it all becomes hysterically funny and I can hardly walk. No; even that is as superficial as I can make it. It gets to the point when one can't be bothered to be intelligent, even to oneself. And isn't this sense of style a very dubious non-quality, a hangover from the nineteenth century really? Almost a weakness of character? I believe it may be. Certainly it makes you lonely.

I'm aware of heavy steps outside, and the doorbell rung sharply as though by a large, padded finger, so that the noise pierces a hole through your head. I open it and there's a man in overalls. Michael's piano has arrived from his old lodgings. Also a cardboard box of scrunched-up paper.

Four men carry the piano into the hall, almost at a run as though they're part of an obstacle race. One man is obviously spokesman for the group because he puffs and pants so noisily you'd think he was doing it for a fee on stage. Where shall they put it? Well, just there right at the back of the hall in the darkness against the wall, until I can ask Father.

When they've gone, I look at the clock. Nearly half-past five. I'm going out tonight; Charles Hamblin, a man I hardly know, phoned me up. I know he's married, and so I shouldn't be going. Why did I say yes? I suppose because I decided to allow myself one gay evening, after the anguish of Michael going to Pakistan and the duties and pressures of life here trying to please Father. That will relieve the tension, one evening of nonsense; it really doesn't matter who it is, so long as he doesn't bicker and pick holes in me. I can get that kind of emotional involvement from my own family. The truth is that my emotions are completely absorbed by Michael and Father, and there's nothing left over. That should be what every married wolf is looking for. How much interest shall I have to take in him? Dare I be myself? For one evening only there's always the chance that we could just enjoy ourselves. Shall I keep down the nightclub vein I have, or shall I, just for one night, make demands? Going to Annabel's with Michael was pure joy; two silky animals, who adored dancing and were not going to harm one another, setting out together. At twenty Michael has a body built to withstand great blasts of electronic pop music that barks or whines or hums, or to drink through his feet the lightest thrown-away melody and muffled words by Herb Alpert; it seems to set his clothes quivering while his face remains pale, immaculate as though he were thinking in his bath. But never snobbish or derisive or inhuman. The married Mr Hamblin will have a good deal to compete with; in this way I've secured for his wife his physical safety. In addition there's a good chance that I shall behave badly, and he'll bring out a 'bruited abroad'. I believe I can risk wearing something really smart.

There's a key scratching around in the lock, and it's my father, home unnaturally early. He calls out:

'Pigeon . . . you there?'

'Yes, Father. Here I am.'

I got to kiss him. His skin is still fresh after a short day. He seems to have many coats on. He puts them in the hall cupboard, and goes to wash. In an instant, he's returned (Father is so *quick*) and says:

'You going out tonight?'

'Yes . . . Is that all right?' (Why not? Why not, for God's sake?)

'Oh, I expect I'll be all right.' (But I didn't ask you, Father, whether you'd be all right.) He smiles at me so kindly; then he makes his mouth into a rather grotesque O and taps the side of it as we used to as children when we imitated the noise of wine being poured from a bottle:

'Do you see that?'

I'm puzzled and look at him. 'Just at the corners there?'

'Yes. Those sores. See them?'

'It's just a bit red.'

'It happens every winter. You know, Pigeon, we must have more fresh vegetables. It's always frozen peas, or frozen corn on the cob. And that's not the same thing.'

I feel numb; so my housekeeping hasn't been good enough. And if I go out tonight, won't that be another mark against me on the domestic balance sheet? It's not as if there's any future in it; not even a kiss, let alone something more. Oh if I'm going to be hung for a lamb, I might as well be hung for a sheep. If he's the slightest bit attractive, this married man of one evening, and if the opportunity comes up, I'll get myself kissed and be hanged.

I always think Father is following me thought by thought. The information seems to be shouting itself out of my head. But no, with that look of reproach on his face he's still brooding over the frozen peas. I say to him:

'I could go round to Mrs Mittler's and get a fresh lettuce straight away, if you like.'

He turns away, irritated that I'm putting myself out when he fully expected me to be selfish and in a hurry to dress myself up for a younger man.

'No, no. That's not the point. It's not a question of one fresh lettuce. It's our daily food consumption.'

He walks into the hall frowning and, preparatory to going upstairs, switches on the light. The piano! Good Lord, if he'd seen that earlier, we wouldn't have needed the frozen peas for our contention.

'What on earth is . . . *this*?'

'Michael's piano. I was going to ask you where we should put it.'

'Where we should put it! I don't want a thing like that in the house. Really, you must be out of your mind. An old-fashioned upright piano! It's hideous!'

'But I've always wanted a piano anyway!'

'If you want a piano, I'll get you a baby grand. But you must get that thing moved out tomorrow. I should sell it. Michael will never use it again.'

'Never use it again! Of course he will!

'Listen, Pigeon. By the time he gets back from his current fad he'll have forgotten all about it. Will you allow me to know best?'

No. Yes. What's the answer to that? Father is peering into the cardboard box now, as if into another world. And yet this is the world of his son, so close, practically his own.

'What on earth are all these dirty bits of paper?' He knows perfectly well what they are. 'You'd better throw it away. We'll have rats nesting in there.'

'Yes, of course.' Of course I shall throw away Michael's worksheets while he's desperately trying to support himself in another country half-way across the world. Father seems appeased. He says mildly in an off-hand manner:

'Just go through them quickly. If there's anything that needs keeping (he doesn't say "that's *worth* keeping") . . . I know I can trust you to do that for Michael.'

'Yes,' I'm bewildered, 'of course I'll do that for Michael.'

'Good, pet.' He kisses me, feeling that something that was previously in a mess has now been cleared up. I only know that a moment ago I was saving Michael's papers from Father, and the next, here he is saving them from me. What a psychologist! For an instant father and son were bolted together in a silent, absolute struggle for power in front of that piano, almost the purest struggle between art and matter. Now it's blown over, the dust has settled, and lo and behold, Father triumphant on the arts side!

When he's at the top of the stairs I call out:

'You've met Charles Hamblin, haven't you?'

'Have I? I don't know.'

'He's married. Do you think I should go out with him?'

'It all depends.' His voice is contented. 'Anyway you know I never interfere in your affairs.' I can hear that he's gone a step further down the passage when he asks sharply: 'Are you taking your car?'

'I can't. It's not working.'

The response comes back as an order.

'Take mine then. The keys are in the hall.'

Father hates me driving his car; if I go on an errand in it and adjust the seat to suit me, and remember to release it afterwards, even then he gets into it suspiciously and listens to the engine as if I've thrown a spanner into it and he's positive that if he listens carefully enough he will hear it clank about. He once said to me craftily about his old car, as though he'd finally summed up the problem: 'Have you been resting your foot on the clutch?' He wanted me to admit I'd been using it as a foot-stool. His new Bentley is fully automatic, has doors as heavy as safe doors from the Bank of England, and a steel body as wide as a ping-pong table. Inside you serve from one comer of it, while burning hot air and noisy radiophonic music try to draw off your attention, subdue, drown and kill you. There is no contact with the outside world through green gymnasium windows. No married man could possibly feel anything but uneasy, inside or outside it. It is indisputably the car that belongs to a powerful, discriminating father, and to try to seduce his daughter in anything less would be madness. Yes, I am possessively loved and protected, and in many ways I'm grateful for it. And after all, Father's car and bed remain as empty as my own. Is that my doing?

He'd rather I drove his car than got into someone else's! And suddenly I realise why there was such a fuss about the piano. He had to prove to himself that I loved him more than I loved Michael, and the piano was an ideal object for the test. In the case of the bits of paper he was going too far and he knew it, but even there he got me to promise I'd throw away some part of them. It's as though he's trying to shut down on certain aspects of his own character, pieces of himself; but, as Goethe said, you can't get rid of something that really belongs to you even if you throw it away. Which is why women can never rid themselves of certain men, and *vice versa*. Those morsels of paper scrunched up by hands trembling with hysteria, ignorance and genius, dirty with the dirt of a Notting Hill Gate lodging house, belong to Father and he knows it. And he wants me to get rid of them for him, and to relieve him of the burden of owing them, because they have no value on any terms whatsoever. They only begin to have value when he wants so much to be rid of them.

2

'This menu isn't large enough. I can still see over the top of it.'

I can see perfectly over the top of it and I'm watching my Wolf in the gloom. He reads every word on his placard carefully, so he must be over thirty-five and doesn't miss anything. As usual I made a lightning decision about the food, which I may regret. He mumbles:

'Not really big enough for a souvenir. You need a table. Would you like to order something?'

The voice is a trifle peremptory and that makes me give the menu back to the waiter at once. It's a nuisance though because now I have to work from memory.

'Cold caviar soup. My blinding passion.'

He laughs shallowly to accommodate this, and goes on with the examination.

'And then?'

I want to be irritating, especially since this is the wrong moment. But he makes me feel I'm back at school. 'Repeal of the Corn Laws' drifts through my head. I look up at him quickly. He's alerted, with hands over the menu as though conducting a miniature orchestra, very grave, formal, waiting for me.

'Oh . . .' in a tone soft and quick enough to conciliate him, but a little too sweet really, almost stuttering my way back into his good graces. 'The pheasant pie sounds excellent. Nothing in between, thanks.'

Thank God that's done. At least he doesn't hang about. And he gets on with the conversation too, that's equally promising. But I have the feeling that he'll tell me off if I *play*. I ask myself quite seriously: 'Does this man *like* me?' I don't think he does. Then why is he here? The answer to that is very simple: I attract him. But I don't think he knows why. And it seems to irritate him. As though I were attracting him for the wrong reasons, and in the middle of a conversation he finds he's not being given his head as he is in fruitful conversations with his wife, and suddenly asks himself why he is there, putting up with it. But I'm also putting up with him. And I haven't had my head once so far this evening. So, to sum up, we're slightly at loggerheads, making life difficult for one another when we have the chance, but overlooking this in the interests of the future which seems to lie there on the table between us like a chessboard . . . where all the mistakes are just waiting to be made (as the great chess master said). The game, in which a mass of decisions and countermoves must be considered at every second, ends in a bedroom or a *cul-de-sac*. But shall we ever get to either? At one moment in the conversation we seem to be entering that bedroom, united, happy, spontaneous. And at the next we're strangers, not even the human strangers who are brought together at the edge of a pavement when the lights change and the traffic moves by, but hostile animals who will either fight bitterly or run away. I suddenly realise that he's been talking *all this time* and has come to the end of a sentence, and wants to be praised or helped! Being inattentive is unforgivable. But I've been admiring him while he was talking; I like the curly hair with grey twists in it, I like the dark pupils with that curious drab dark green in them exactly like my own, he has an intellectual's undeveloped shoulders and beautiful lanky body (like Michael's), and a curiously strong, perfect round neck, perhaps from turning his head so often to find out what's going on at the next table; he's doing it right now! It seems a pity not to tell him how attractive he is, but of course I can't risk it, and say:

'But you don't really notice what you eat, do you, seriously? It doesn't mean a thing to you.'

He's very pleased with this accurate and very ordinary piece of character revelation, and hoping that there is something even more succulent attached to it, asks a leading question:

'How did you know?'

'By the way you ordered, as though rattling off a formula in answer to an equation.' (Although in fact, the answer is, no one with those delicate shoulders is ever interested in food. Sex, yes; food, *never*.)

'Formula?' He's going to pick me up on the word 'formula'; I shall never kiss him in a thousand years. He's trying to get me to qualify what I've said: horrid little pedant. I turn my head away and say sulkily, without interest:

'I expect it's like stockbroking. You think of a number and then double it.'

That's a definite rupture, rude and not funny. I wait for him to lean back, interlock his fingers and say carefully: 'Ah.' No, he's still there, close to the edge of the table, keeping the thread going. He says:

'Yes?'

'And then you get your caviar soup' . . . because the waiter has just put mine down in front of me. It's the same colour as the windows of Father's car, and cold. As I sip it, I know it's my turn to show goodwill by starting up a fresh conversation. I'd like to understand this man. I wonder if he'll give me time. I say adventurously, but seriously:

'Charles . . .'

He looks at me, astounded by my daring. I've never pronounced his Christian name before and I'm almost expecting him to tell me sternly that I've gone too far. But today doesn't everyone call everyone else by a Christian name from the instant of meeting? Perhaps he wanted a formal refrigerated flirtation, but in that context we would have to have real conversations – and very likely on his subject! And surely at this stage, even in England, isn't he supposed to take more interest in me than I in him? Or am I hopelessly out of date?

I ask him about his friendships and his work. He gives me the normal replies; that he has about two close friends, and that he doesn't like stockbroking very much but hated being poor while he was at Oxford. I try to collect the information he's given me into an epigram of some sort, to amuse him. But instead he takes it personally, and says:

'Oh, that's a cut!'

So we're at cross purposes again, due to my brand of conversational playing, which simply doesn't suit him. I eat two mouthfuls of pheasant pie in silence, and then a tiny white new potato with speckles of green on it. I swallow the potato, and for a moment it hurts. I feel like crying with disappointment. I can see the manila folders filled with accounts lying on the table waiting for me tomorrow. And an oblong envelope with air-mail patterns and insignia on it from Michael. I find myself saying crossly:

'These potatoes are lumpy.' It's exactly my father's tone, and you can't ignore it. For the first time this evening, my Wolf is at a disadvantage, due entirely to the authority in a certain tone of voice. He responds and conciliates me.

'We'll send them back at once. They do look rather lumpy.' They don't. 'I'm sorry.'

So this is how my father feels when I beg his forgiveness for mistakes made in the kitchen; smug and self-righteous.

'These potatoes are simply appalling.' There he goes to a waiter who nods, and would nod to anything, like Frank Sinatra.

We're eating in one of the most expensive restaurants in London, noted for an excellent menu, and someone is bound to emerge from the background and talk over those potatoes. What a pity neither of us has the slightest interest in food; potatoes, too, so basic, like blankets on a bed, a part of a meal that doesn't really count. But it's always a large grey potato that gets lodged inside the top of your chest while turning a dangerous corner under the breastbone, so perhaps one should talk about them occasionally. Indigestion begins with a potato.

My Wolf has suddenly begun to talk about women he admires; women in the news, women who write, women in society. His voice is light, and it seems to move quickly, so that in a minute or so the conversation is thickly crammed with women. I'm asked to admire X because she is so intelligent and has genuine insight (when he says 'insight' I can see Michael, just out of potato range, making grimaces at me in the shadows at the back of my mind); I do so grumpily. He immediately brings up Y because she has such a sweet nature. My own nature blackens and deteriorates; I feel sour and malevolent. Yes, I agree with him, she has a sweet nature, it's undoubtedly true. And now here's Z, don't I think she's pretty? It's too much, the insight and the sweet nature were more than enough, but if one woman doesn't admit another woman is pretty she's always written off as a 'bitch'. How do I know whether Z is pretty? Why on earth should I make a physical effort to see Z with his eyes? He's waiting, quite eagerly, for me to say one bitchy thing. He's even smiling slightly, something he hasn't done before. The conversation really interests him. The point is that I'm concentrating hard on his head and shoulders across the table, and don't have any opinions at all, not one. Certainly not about other women. Do I know any? I know myself, my aunts and Michael's girl friends, some of whom I like very much. So why on earth should I be goaded into saying something like: 'They all look alike to me,' which is trite and which I don't mean?

The thought flashes through my head that the motive behind such a conversation is to spur me to do some action or to make some statement which would not normally be mine, in an attempt to 'prove' myself. I seem to have been placed first in intellectual competition, then in moral competition, and finally in physical competition with a number of entirely unknown women. It's highly disagreeable. I sponge all expression off my face and just sit there. I really feel unhappy, and wish he'd talk about himself, which would be much more interesting.

A waiter has rolled a double-deck trolley to an awkward

position just behind my right arm. I need a driving mirror to make a proper choice. Very well, stewed compote, those brown pears in brown pear liquid, to go with the conversation. If possible, served on a brown plate.

I cut into them with my spoon and eat gloomily. A hand comes down and covers them with squalid cream; with it comes a babble of waiters' conversation. Of course we're lucky to have been allowed to talk to one another at all, my Wolf and I, because normally waiters take the lion's share of the conversation. It's so irritating that a few seconds later . . . we're smiling at one another over the tablecloth! More hands appear and snatch up this and that at random, with a clattering noise. I try to hold down an ashtray – at least, it's a little silver bowl – but with a sharp tug they get it away from me. The interference is unbelievable; at one moment I have an impression that the aggressive waiters will strip us down to our underwear if we go on sitting there. No; here's a superior creature bringing a flask of hot coffee *in silence*. The calm is exceedingly pleasant, it's like being washed up on a desert island after a terrible stormy night with radio transmitters going non-stop in pidgin English. We look over our shoulders nervously, to make sure we really are alone. This joining of forces against a common enemy is fatal, it's an aphrodisiac. My Wolf looks at me appreciatively. I feel myself glowing; the good food is working on both of us. What were we talking about? I've forgotten. A feeling of well-being envelopes us. I like this man, and he likes me. I suddenly realise that I haven't been trying to know him on any level except the physical one; the rest of the time I've been either provocative or defensive. Oh – for a moment I'd forgotten he was married, so I can't afford to get to know him. What is happening, of course, is that I'm getting to know him badly, through a series of mental obstacles I've erected for us both to fall over, and which are entirely false, and to which he, in turn, is reacting with false characteristics. Meanwhile I'm getting fond of him. Why? Because he's there. So that's how you get to know someone you're not allowed to know.

Now we have to leave the table, our security, an island with a lamp on it, where we've just made a truce. We struggle to get rid of our napkins, the size of sheets. The moment we stand up, we're strangers again and cross the restaurant together like any other imitation couple, embalmed in wholly different alcohols. Some women try to vary this slow exit towards the open forest by actually speaking to the man they're with. This terrifies a man and he automatically says 'What?' I'm curious to know what mine is doing. He's . . . humming! Good Lord, then he isn't sophisticated. What a good thing – or is it? Perhaps it's my presence that makes him do it. We're nervous with one another, that's why we pick on the wrong things to say. But I hadn't realised before that he was quite *so* nervous. Almost as nervous as I am myself. Fortunately all my energy goes on walking well; Father hates women who knock up against tables . . . ('and shoulders a little bit rounded, please').

There's the street – these London streets that Michael adores; he says he only feels really well on the nights when the city settles down to a cold dish of fog. My Wolf walks silently beside me. I have no idea what's going on in his mind. Probably nothing. One must never assume other people's minds bear any relation to one's own. I ask quietly:

'Do you know where your car is?'

'Yes. It's here.'

We're beside it. And I left Father's car a street or two away because I couldn't find a space. I offer to walk to it; after all the evening is over. With off-hand courtesy (almost sharply) my Wolf says:

'Jump in. I'll take you.'

Once inside, he takes hold of the steering wheel, and just as I think he's going to start the car, he says to me in profile:

'Yes.' He laughs slightly. What a surprise!

For a second I'm thrown. Then I go back twelve years, and remember that if the boy who took you out didn't start the car at once, it was because he wanted to embrace you and didn't know how to do it. My Wolf gets younger and younger. I try to remember what I would have done twelve years ago; so many people have come and gone since then, but the scratches have only been superficial. I was absorbed in bringing Michael up. 'You must smoke,' I tell myself. Of course, that was what smoking was for. I open the little shagreen cigarette case Father once gave to me – it's like a piece of a Roman bathroom floor – and inside are one whole Nazionale cigarette and one half, burnt but carefully restored (a Soho habit, picked up from Michael), plus a folded slip of paper, like a prescription.

'What's that?' asks my Wolf, leaning over.

I've never seen his head so close before, and it frightens me with all that hair on it. I catch a flash from the eyes – much too close – really shiny and polished like marbles with warm enamel centres.

'Oh, it's a declaration of love I once had. I keep it in case I never get another.' That was provocative, but I can only plead that it's true.

I take it out from beneath the soft dingy-white body of the Italian cigarette and hand it to him. In doing so I touch his hand fractionally; it's icy, clammy-cold.

He unwraps the prescription and reads it, leaning away towards his window. I know the words on that piece of paper; it's a restaurant chit and it says: 'Miss, ai love yu.' He refolds it, so that the message is hidden again, out of respectful sympathy for the original masculine writer. Then he gives it back to me.

I'm smoking, and I know that it's my duty to talk. I also know that the more I talk, the more nervous he'll get. If I put him out of humour with himself on the other side of a restaurant table, I'm bound to enrage him while seated *à côté* in a motor car. Although he gives me jerky answers, he really *tries* to talk. An enormous prairie opens out between us, and across great distances which increase minute by minute we communicate, gradually taking to the telephone and making a great effort to hammer the message across. But even so his voice keeps getting blotted out – at this great distance – and when I can snatch at the sense, I do so, and reply immediately, as in a transatlantic call. During all this time, and it seems endless, he glances at me twice, but naturally I look away, horrified that he should try to catch my eye when we are managing perfectly well by telephone.

Looking back on this final piece of communication, I see nothing that could have stopped it except sunrise. As it was, I put a lighted cigarette into the thick black fur along the bottom of my maxi-coat, and had to jump out of the car. My Wolf remained inside. All the best London streets are supplied with gleaming puddles. I've always admired them because the water changes colour, and now I know what they're for.

I dip the fur into a purple one, squeeze the water out as if out of a little bath sponge, and get back into the car.

My Wolf boyishly puts out his arm as though to help me in, but quickly lays my head against his chest and his mouth against my hair. Oh! I'm dazed by the elegance and thought contained in the attack. So his intelligence is in his gestures. That's where it is. I lie still like a nervous domestic bird that's caught, that wanted to be caught, but is afraid by habit. Meanwhile I close my eyes and half go to sleep. What an exhausting evening. My lids fall as though they'll never rise again. We have nearly thirty seconds of opium-deep sleep. But my Wolf is travelling over my features with his, perhaps to get me accustomed to them. I'm dazed and astounded to feel another face so close to mine, so soft and friendly, and his cheeks and hair are fragrant. I can hardly remember, as this face gently touches mine, which of my features are which, everything seems equal. I've just decided, from my slumber, that I certainly shan't kiss him, when the travelling face descends still further, and the dangerous mouth, which only two hours ago was saying: 'Formula?' is finally level with my own.

I don't care. I really don't care. All I have to do is to retain my physical good manners. I'm not really afraid. I trust my ability to extemporise, which is almost the only skill I possess. If he kisses me badly, I'll never let him know it. And in my present mood, I may not know it either. And even while I'm thinking this (and how annoyed he'd be that I was thinking it) his mouth, which turns out to be dry, is very slowly and patiently and drily eating at mine.

In an instant I know infallibly that I'm with a wise lover and that I'm being told to wait. I'm being told to wait as if he'd taken the watch off my wrist, and said: 'Now *I'll* tell you when to do things. Don't tell *me.*' And so out of respect, and obediently, I wait, not relaxed but tense, breathing deeply, and forgetting that waiting is the most dangerous game in the world because it creates a crisis inside a crisis and rapidly becomes uncontrollable. So that in a moment I'm almost impelled to cry out: 'I can't wait,' and my married Wolf replies with his mouth: 'You *must.*' And when absolutely on edge I feel, a whole year later, the tongue that lives inside this accomplished mouth, I'm nearly done for – and so is he. Because he's put forth his hands to hold me on either side of my waist, and they're trembling so violently that a second time I'm filled with overwhelming respect for a head so clever, patient, and controlled, which is being given away by a pair of trembling hands, and which is, even so, succeeding.

A kiss so well started and so much desired has a powerful life, very difficult to break off. We're grown up, we don't forget to breathe, and no time is wasted. Now this kiss has to be long enough to tell me what I want to know, but not too long or it turns into an engulfment. But first kisses, it seems to me at the moment, have a special licence of their own, and they take full advantage of it. So I kiss longer than I'm allowed to, and find out that my Wolf's body is immensely, rhythmically strong, and when the palm of my hand is stretched out flat, meeting the palm of his, there's a declaration, a spasm of decisive magic, which announces to me: 'This man will be your lover' . . . and also that he's going to behave quite badly . . . I break off immediately, surprised that I'm surprised. Haven't I been calling him a wolf? So why am I in the least put out? Did I really think I had made friends with him? Oh no; he'd only made himself my friend for a short while, and now, breathing quietly in the gloom, he returns to himself. I keep close to his head, hoping by doing so to retain its friendship. It moves off a little and says very softly, rather mournfully:

'You twist what I say, you know.'

This is true, of course, and I've taken immense pains over it during the evening, but only because he attracts me. Otherwise I wouldn't even bend it; to twist what someone else is saying is the first sign of serious involvement. And surely he wouldn't want anything less? In the same tone I reply: 'I know,' astonished that he hadn't realised how difficult it was to do, and that it's a compliment. And then, really sorry that it annoyed him: 'I'm sorry.'

He accepts the apology, and lowers his head and offers it to me as though he wants it petted. Father doesn't like me to pet his head, so it's a long time since I've had a head offered to me, and I touch the warm wool with care and interest. Presently it says improbably:

'Will you come and sleep with me in Ireland?'

I hadn't expected that, and the immediate polite social answer is: 'But of course.' In any case it doesn't really matter what I answer to such an ill-judged question, so I say peevishly:

'What for?'

I start to get out of a car I've been in far too long. My Wolf at once presses the self-starter. The car is now all movement, lights go on, a heater hums, a radio deafens us: 'And now, folks . . . !' I find my cigarette case on the floor, and then put on my dark glasses which have lenses in them. I at once feel safe, although they darken the darkness. I could drive a capsule to the moon in them, as though all my nerves were protected from moonlight by a layer of smoked glass.

My Wolf has buckled himself in with a seat-belt. I don't take this bourgeois gesture seriously, and start to laugh because Michael has always taught me that you're conditioned by such actions and they run right through your life, even down to the way you write letters and mix a drink: 'And you lose your poetry.' When Father does up his seat-belt, he intends to do a hundred miles an hour down an autostrada. That's high Philistia in action and rates as poetry. But not only is my Wolf serious, he offers *me* a seat-belt as though it's the most natural thing in the world. How can a man behave so conventionally (how *can* he be such a drip), after kissing so unconventionally and throwing in an Irish spree into the bargain? In order not to offend someone I've been so close to, I try to speak his language and bring out this sentence:

'I belong to the school that thinks they're dangerous because you can't get out of them quickly.'

He says nothing (sulking already?) and drives around looking for the Bentley. There it is, really enormous sideways. It's like that whale in the Cousteau underwater film. I'm never cowed by a large machine when I'm allowed to run it myself, and get out readily. There is no final embrace, he doesn't even touch my hand. But looks at the car curiously.

'You don't find it too large to handle?'

I'm struggling with a gleaming door, which is stiff.

'No. Not really.' Ah, got it open at last. 'This is only the female, you know. The male's much bigger.'

On hearing this he salutes me without smiling, and drives away at a moderate speed, leaving me with a sensation of failure.

For a moment, only a moment, I slump in the driver's seat. Where are the roses, the gentle courtship, the glances full of love? Until now I had assumed he must be unhappily married or else he wouldn't have asked me out. But for the first time it occurs to me he could be happily married and all that's left over after that is an appetite for additional sex and a bullying to get it. That must be why the behaviour around that kiss was so carefully proscribed; there was no spilling-over of intermediate kisses, nothing loose or wanton like that. On the contrary, he seemed at one moment to cringe away in case I 'started something up' on my own. Unless I canter straight into that loose-box in Ireland when the command is given, not before and not after, I shall be brushed off as unworthy of the magnificence, the uniqueness and the intensity of his sexual desire for me.

I make the Bentley murmur, and then realise I haven't got my driving glasses. Still, I direct the large, elegant bonnet along the moonlit roads quite well. My Wolf's kiss is still on my damaged mouth; there's no comfort in it, but I've learnt a great deal while trying not to give myself away to him, naturally enough. I wanted to find out his time-sequences and his actual morality, as against the morality of the times, which he might have assumed. The disconcerting thing about a moment of absolute attraction between two people is that it's so exhilarating it lasts *forever* – unless it's killed by bad manners, of course. They'd kill anything. Oh I'm cold and thirsty and lonely.

3

'Your French is awful, you don't work at it, Pigeon. You've got a wooden head.'

'It's only because yours is so fluent and you give all the orders. But I can do other things.'

'Then I wish you'd do something about your clothes. Look at that French family over there. And now have a look at your anorak.'

'Father! Don't nag me on a mountain top.'

'I'm not nagging you. I'm just trying to get you to pull yourself together, and make something of yourself. You know, Pigeon, you're pathetic.'

Father looks marvellous; his sweater is navy-blue with a fine red pencil-line around the neck. Behind him I can see the top of the mountain, very sharp and covered with brilliant, glossy icing. It's so steep that I don't know how they managed to set up this café complete with deck-chairs. After only three days' skiing Father has a boy's blond tan. His citrus-coloured goggles are pushed up above the famous eyebrows and he leans across to my deck-chair in the bright sunlight, smiling at me. Then he very gently writes with his finger on my face (I can just feel the tip of his nail), going from my nose down to the corner of my mouth.

'You've got a line down there,' he says, as matter-of-fact as a doctor.

'Oh . . . but at thirty, is that dreadful?'

'Well, it just means you're not as young as you were.' He smiles at me with even greater kindness, while closing the door on any sort of future with this sentence.

At first I don't really take in what he's said, the sun is so bright up here that I'm smiling back at him, until I suddenly realise what the words mean and who has said them to me, and then my inner world suddenly collapses. It's like a raft made of planks going under in brown water. And I suppose my face caves in expressively, because I see him reacting to it, and he says irritably:

'Don't *cry*. It makes you look old.'

'I'm sorry.' My face caves in even further, my forehead tightens, which makes it look puckered on the outside, and I'm shaken by sobs but keep them in at the centre of my body. 'I know it's ugly. It was just that you took me by surprise. It was such a tough thing to say. You don't mean it, do you?'

'No, of course not.' He puts his hand over mine with the old affection. 'It's just that I want you to make the best of yourself. And sometimes I don't think you try.'

'But . . . in the evenings I dress well, don't I?'

'Yes.' He thinks back, and nods. 'You're very smart in the evenings. But your general attire during the daytime, and your hair –'

'But I've been skiing! I've had it under my cap!'

'That doesn't make the slightest difference if it's glossy and well cared for.'

I hang my head. He's not proud of me, and I'm so proud

of him. Perhaps I am badly dressed, but in that case I need a larger allowance and more time to go with it. Running one house is quite easy, but converting a second house on the other side of London takes up all the slack. Father wanted the direction of the staircase changed to make the sitting-room larger, a wall knocked down, and two new bathrooms. All these structural alterations have to be carefully imagined and tested in the mind, just as that kiss with my Wolf was, in a sense, imagined in advance. So that, physically, when altering a building or kissing a strange man, you only go just as far as you have imagined in your mind. The main thing is to find someone who imagines at the same rate and to the same depth. And now it turns out I've got a dirty anorak on, simply because I've been trying to please two men who can't be pleased! Good heavens, dressing well is easy enough. It just means being a little bit more selfish and not lending out your imagination for other projects.

My father's criticism always throws me off balance, because it's so unexpected. I always think he *must* be on my side; and then suddenly, out of the blue, he isn't! But the curious thing about being hurt by your own father is that you never for a moment doubt that you're loved, or that it's for your own good. Half a minute's crying, and then it's over and forgotten forever; children adore their parents and are incapable of bearing malice. He has absolute power over me, and I think about pieces of his behaviour for hours at a time in order to understand him.

'What time is your lesson?' He looks at his watch.

'Four-thirty.'

'You'd better hurry then, hadn't you? It's no good me paying for lessons if you don't take advantage of them.'

I get up like a child of thirteen, full of shame. My hands are curled up like a child's too, the fingers of my gloves are soggy with hard knots of wool. Paid for, in a dirty anorak, with hair that isn't glossy, I feel my eyes glisten again. Father observes it, and looks away. There's a dark young woman near the ski-lift about my age, dressed in a new white plastic ski-suit; she has a vizor with steel dots at the sides, and seems to be smiling all the time – one wonders why. Father looks back at me, pulls down his goggles, forces a smile and says:

'Off with you then!'

On the way down in the lift, seated among healthy young people with a brown crust on their faces, I make a quick search for lines from nose to chin. Everybody's got them. You can't have a face without them. That little girl can't be more than eleven, and she's got a line any father could be proud of. She's certainly not as young as she was at nine. I'm greatly reassured.

At the hotel, I go up to my room to collect the French grammar books, and my skates . . . because there might still be time, after the lesson. Father's sister, my aunt Zoë, is with us in the hotel. I call her Zoë, but never call my father Daddy. I suppose because he has so much authority and because I respect him so deeply; and subconsciously, I like to add to those aspects of his character which give me safety, and not diminish them by pet names. I know inwardly I'm still too nervous to live my own life and have to go on living his for the moment. And yet it's he who makes me nervous. And so he calls me Pigeon and I remain thirteen. But I'm just beginning to find out that the only real happiness comes from living your own life. And it was Michael who took mine away from me!

There's the letter from my Wolf on top of the French books. It's warm-hearted; I hadn't allowed for that. I had it with my breakfast in bed this morning, and Father came in in the middle and tried to read it over my shoulder. It now occurs to me with absolute certainty that this was the reason Father attacked my clothes. He doesn't like a letter from an admirer following me to a Swiss hotel. He instantly tried to put me out of action by suggesting I wasn't 'good enough'. Bad French, dirty anorak, dull hair; really, a hopeless case. As it happens, I couldn't have been more surprised than he was when the letter arrived. I never expected to see my Wolf again. After all, there was and is no certainty that he will ever get me to bed; I was horribly natural – didn't flatter him and said what I thought into the bargain. I'm told that everybody else goes straight to bed; but although I'm told this, I don't know anyone who actually does it. But it's only women who instinctively know what love-making can be, and know also that they can only give and receive it from certain kinds of men, who impose a check on behaviour and a time interval. It's only women who know what immorality of behaviour is who are moral; so that caution should be looked upon as a signal from a voluptuary, the highest danger signal there is. And fathers should keep their young daughters well away from the moral woman who *could* teach them everything, and leave them in the company of the promiscuous who are physically illiterate. I put the letter in my pocket and hurry downstairs, laughing to myself at this amiable piece of logic.

I'm late. I have the money for the lesson in my other zip-pocket, but I haven't finished the exercises I was given to do yesterday. I know my tutor, Monsieur Secker, will take the next step too fast and I shall have to improvise, groping after facts I don't yet know, and speaking above or below the actual meaning I intend. I loathe the false emotional proportions which are the result of not knowing a language thoroughly. Isn't it just as immoral, illiterate, as the promiscuity I have described? My dear Wolf Charles, you must get the emotional proportions right if you want us to speak the same language physically.

I hurry along the edge of the lake with its stiff blue grass. I don't like passing the Alsatian dogs, especially the ones with a lot of black in their dog coats.

These steep white frozen roads are devils to negotiate. They're just cambered slabs of hard white glass, not a mark on them. I arrive at the house and mount to the first floor. He's always waiting for me, very courteous and dead, with one wall eye – it has a blue-white wall over it like the roads – and something seemingly wrong with another part of his body, but I can't be sure whether it's an arm or a leg.

We start. He lets nothing pass. I pronounce and pronounce, but when my mouth tries too hard it can do nothing. True mimicry comes from the mind. He is totally disinterested. It appears that in the past he has only ever had brilliantly clever students who put together sentences in the correct grammar, greyly and without sweating or flamboyance. A curious thing about this room of his is that once I'm inside it, all words are equal, and all information is equal. If I read with feeling he indicates – I think just by not moving the grey hand with its clean grey nails that holds his copy of the text – he indicates that I am a bestial peasant, at the mercy of the flowing of my blood.

We have colourless exchanges, only coming to life a little when we are well back in the past. Yes, back in classical Athens, if the reference is absolutely correct and preferably of an unliterary nature, we may warm up slightly.

It isn't that he places himself, mentally, in a superior position to myself, no. We are absolutely equal, even though master and student, except that on his side there is an enormous, silent, specialised lump sum of knowledge, and on mine there are a few phrases, bits and pieces irrelevant to any whole, candle-ends, just nothing.

The difficulty is that after a while the intellectual equality on other levels breaks down under the solid weight of that lump sum. And while I am in this room, I seem not to know even those things I know: my own name, who I am. And out of the whole of my enormous knowledge of literature gained through teaching Michael, if some were to ask me what I know, I would answer: 'Nothing.' Monsieur Secker manages to give me a little grey information, dry as a bone, and I, who am panting and thirsting after knowledge, who could eat up Dante, Nietzsche, Verga, Zola, in four gulps, am only just able to take in some particles imperfectly, and possibly ruining them almost at once by the flow of passion with which my mind appropriates them and makes them into its own creatures.

When I take my leave of him, I could crash down on the ice outside, dead.

I come out, tamed and stinging; resolute; with my imagination dry and stale as old (but still nourishing) bread. Instead of dropping from the extreme mental fatigue of maintaining myself on a level where I have not the information to make a single perfected move without assistance (it isn't an *exalted* level, but, as you will have guessed, purely concerned with the trivialities of everyday chatter; the density of ideas in Brahms would be child's play after this inhuman stratum where nothing but factual intelligence will do) I feel cleaned out and stronger. My perspectives on ordinary life seem to be in perfect order. I observe things in my head, as outside on the road, very exactly. I don't see life as being either hard or easy, but only as being there. I no longer avoid people's eyes, and walk back along the ice with cold cheeks and a vast, warm, empty dark head in which the new information is being enjoyed. The Alsatians brush by me and I walk into them fearlessly, half wolf myself, psychologically *entre chien et loup*.

It's six o'clock, getting dark.

Here's the great lake again, the Moubra, now covered with *French* glass. I walk on the luminous slabs. It will thaw shortly; broken windows go down to the bottom, which is solid. I have my skates over my shoulder, with the long laces tied together. I sit down and rapidly change into them, pushing my foot around a corner into the difficult boot-shape until it goes home, zonk. Then the lacing is criss-crossed up the brass studs; a double flip round at the top, and an evenly tied bow. I stand up. No one about. I have the lake to myself. Excellent. What luck!

The surface is treacherous because smaller blocks of ice

are strewn about, frozen to it, and under the powdering of snow you can't always see them. Every now and then, you come on a skating floor from which the snow has been swept away, and then you look right down through the ice and you can see pockets of raw white air and dark champagne spawn lying in a double rain, bolted up inside the glass tablets. Some of these skating floors are dark like the tops of shiny dining-room tables, and as you look in through the ice beams, while gliding over them in a state of peaceful exhilaration, you ponder on the depth and total silence.

I'm approaching the centre of the lake. Suddenly there's a sound from far away beneath me; a massive broken grunt is nosing its way up towards me – once, twice! It's as powerful as an intestine or a soul, this sound from the ice age, and it makes water of your sinews as you stand there on your skates, terrified.

Stock-still in the half dark, I listen, as dogs listen, with the whole body, to hear which way the sound will go through the floors below me. In my imagination I can see a great dark table of ice capsize and up-end itself while I slither off the shiny polished surface at the other side.

Like an insect captured with staring, open eyes, I slowly begin to float my body over the grunting, leaving a shaky scripture behind me on the ice. I move on the surface, no longer trusting it, not daring to look at the shore, or indeed anywhere except at the deceptive powder directly in front of me. Gradually, I get myself away from the centre of the music – now it grumbles with its old testament murmur directly behind me. And now I'm bent into the wind, cutting the ground with my skates, one, two, with an increasing venom, as the paralysed fear of the insect gives way to the red-blooded animal which knows how to fly for its life, balanced on two knives.

Thud! I'm into the bank. As my skates hit the grass, I fling myself down on it and lie there panting. I'm convulsed with merriment, just as babies are, all about nothing – listen to that noise in the distance, it's like an old wardrobe cupboard creaking! The Moubra speaks to me! What's this sticking into my ribs? It's the sharp corner of my Wolf's letter. How pleasant and funny civilisation is with its sharp-cornered letters from touchy, spoilt, warm-hearted men. What's going to bed? Why, it's nothing. I'll do it tomorrow, with this new life I've just brought off the lake. I feel as though I've got the whole of the lighted London restaurant in this pocket of mine, complete with silly menus, candles, and sex cricket match. And, besides, it's always the unsuitable men who actually do the love-making these days.

When I get up, my legs wobble. Ah, I really was afraid. Where are the French books and my boots? I look for them along the frosted banks in the dark, find them, and walk fast to the hotel.

I run straight into Zoë outside the lift downstairs. She gives me one of her bolting-eye looks, and I realise that I'm back with the hair and anorak routine. To my astonishment, I suddenly stand my ground and stare back at her. She's just opened her mouth to correct me, and I can even see her uneven bottom teeth, when she's stopped by my face. I can see it myself, reflected in the hall mirror, a carmine mouth shut firmly and very bright eyes. She says mildly:

'We'll be in the bar, when you've changed.'

That's better. Zoë isn't married; she's always fashionably dressed and perfectly finished off. She has a lot of sloping flesh as white as a piece of Chanel No. 5 soap, a completely solid low bosom; she has great charm of manner, a selfish little profile and is mercenary. We all have this straight brown-black hair (except for Michael); hers shines. She has a large private income, runs charities and a protection scheme for the National Trust, and wears rouge.

I brush my own hair and tug it away from my healthy face. With my new strength I put on a purple velvet maxi-skirt I've been holding in reserve, and then a white Courrège tunic. Finally, a churchy cross in purple stones shaped like a kiss and looking wicked: *la croix du mal.* I take time, and mentally I can see Father looking at his watch. When I go down to dinner, I'm stately and rebellious. Father actually *gets up* as I join them. He kisses me on the cheek, possessively. You'd never think I had wept before him on a mountain top only hours ago.

'Here she is!' Nothing about my being late.

We all three go into dinner, united and formidable.

What a scene of rich, quiet feasting. Everything seems to have a fitted carpet; the trolleys, the plates, the conversations. And yet I notice that although we are all eating and talking hard and continuously, the emphasis has been taken out as bones are removed from a body. No one here cares too much about any one cause. There are chandeliers of the whitest ice above us. Zoë asks:

'And what is Michael doing now?'

Father puts down his glass. There's a shadow down from his nose across his face like the shadow from the mountain; he looks obstinate and disappointed, won't reply and glances at me. I don't want to reply either. Why do members of a family have to explain and justify one another so often? I must give her some acceptable bourgeois answer which can be translated into terms of cheque-books and standards of living.

'He's selling commercial television to the Pakistanis.' (He's living off a publisher's advance so as to save himself from people like us.)

'What a good idea. But haven't they got it already?'

'I don't know how advanced it is. But he's an excellent organiser.'

'Is he?' asks Father, interested.

'Of course he is. Think of the amount of advance organisation you need just to write one poem.'

'On a dirty piece of paper,' says Father, friendly, playing the game, and with me, but unable to resist a dig.

'Yes,' says Zoë, 'but people really want to get away from all this kitchen-sink poetry these days. It simply means the culture is becoming decadent.'

Even Father is silent; is it worth going on? Her sensibility seems to have stopped in the fifties; I suppose writing cheques destroyed it. Again I have that inner flash of Michael touching lepers in Karachi – it's a ludicrous picture, but it will recur. And it makes me answer coldly:

'Have you ever read anything Michael's written, Zoë?'

'I've never been allowed to.'

'Well, how on earth do you know it's kitchen-sink? Is Dante the kitchen sink of thirteenth-century Italy?'

'Oh – Dante.' She looked at me severely. 'I hope you're reading him in Italian. The translations are *appalling*.'

'But why do you want me to read him at all?'

'What an extraordinary question!' She looks at Father, as though I'm incorrigible. 'Knowing Dante is an essential part of your education, if you want me to state the obvious.'

'My moral education? You mean the education of my soul?'

She pats my hand and laughs at me.

'Of course, your moral education. Your education on every level. That's why Dante is so marvellous, because he has everything.'

'Is he great because he took on the moral burdens of his time or because he "has everything"?'

Father can see the red light, and clears his throat to interrupt us. But I'm determined to get her to admit that her reasons for admiring Dante are purely in the nature of a good social investment.

'Don't get so carried away! He's great because thousands of people have decided for many different reasons that he is.' She tries to keep it light.

'But it's *your* reason that interests me. The reason at makes Dante great and Michael kitchen-sink.'

'Michael has to prove himself.'

'How can he if you dismiss him before you've even read him? That's immoral. Is that what one learns from Dante?'

'No. From life,' says Father with humour but sharply. But he underrates Zoë, who is more than capable – after all, she sprung the trap in the first place, and she's unruffled:

'Well you *did* say he was selling commercial television to the Pakistanis, and I must say I hadn't realised that that was "taking on the moral burdens of his time".'

Another clear win for the Philistines.

She laughs heartily in my face. '*Core un marmo*', says Dante, heart of marble. And nasty dark rouge the colour of red geraniums.

We all rise and leave the table. I've behaved unforgivably in raising my voice and taking an undue interest in one subject in preference to another. For that is all it amounts to in their eyes. And yet Michael has taken his soul in his hands and tried to make a life with it. But don't imagine I protected him for this reason, not for a minute. I did so because he frightened me with his talk of leprosy and sores. Not one of the three of us around that table cares tuppence for Michael's integrity.

The curious thing about the conversation Father and Zoë have after dinner is that it always seems to be exactly the same one, in England or in Switzerland. An exchange of information about where one buys things, obtains tickets, takes dogs etc. As I drift off to sleep between them, the words grow louder and louder, until, just as I plunge deeply, they shout at the tops of their voices, like two Red Queens who'll do anything to keep you awake. Ultimately all you can hear is: 'Yah! Yah! Yah!'

We fly back to London at the end of the week.

4

When you're at home too much you follow the same thoughts around the same rooms; or, even worse, you pick up the thoughts you had the day before yesterday, the ones you left on the oak chest, there, between the unread open book of *Ethical Studies*, the liqueur bottles and the daffodils which are now dying . . . Oh yes, I remember now, Michael wanted me to go and call on Leo Johnson, a friend of his, and pick up a book of Italian poetry stolen from him. His letter said that the loss of this book was making him ill. There was a hole in his mind where it should be, and every time his thoughts came on it, they fell in and everything went black for about two hours while he tried to remember the exact content of the book, right down to the title page, by developing and printing photographs of it in his memory.

I take the dried-up brown paper flowers out to the kitchen; I actually *hurry* because inwardly I can hear Father's voice saying: 'Those flowers have been dead a week,' i.e. two days; as long as that thought about Michael which is now just as shrivelled up. To get that book means driving up to Hampstead. I'll go at once. It's three o'clock.

I get myself into the same black maxi-coat with the

Nazionale burn in the fur, quenched by purple water. Oh, that kiss! After all that waiting! Such an excellent warm, rounded, sexy tongue. I put my forehead against the lintel of the door for a moment, overcome by my involuntary physical response. A good kiss, like a good book or a good play, lasts for months, years. Some words come back to me, which I'd entirely forgotten and which were uttered by my Wolf immediately afterwards: 'You're dangerous.' Thank heavens for that: it would be appalling not to be dangerous.

Quickly into the car! Before all the sexual moves of that evening are recovered by various parts of my body, as I send the dreams around my veins from my brow which is taking on the impression of the wooden architrave in dents. As it is, my hand has already lifted itself up and has begun a half-caress on the door, and is even now resting on the brass handle so gently, so *incredibly* gently, in a way that makes me frightened for myself.

This old car of mine, which I love, is a beaten-up AC. She's the one thing in the world that I own, and every journey in her is a crisis. My love is founded on realities; she goes faster than anything else on the road of comparable size. She coughs, breathes hoarsely, explodes, and in every way completes the necessary badness of my character. I understand every note of her charming engine. She allows me to be young and bad-mannered. Insults flow out of the window from the driving seat, but I keep breathy and classical: '*Merde*!' Every mood of my father's is played to the general public through my feet on this remarkable machine with its gears that live in silk.

Hampstead. Now just up and down these hilly roads. I

have to park at an unhappy angle as in a bad dream, due to these up and down intellectuals' houses. Michael calls this the middle-aged University of Hampstead. Outside, some milk bottles are ready to topple over.

'Who is it?'

It's very dark at the top of the stairs.

'Arabella. Michael's sister.'

'*Who*? Come in.'

Leo Johnson is in old-fashioned striped flannel pyjamas; they're properly done up, thank God, and complete with buttons and cords. On bare feet he leads the way into a large room filled with more dirty scrunched-up pieces of paper and a bed. It's hot in there. He flings himself down on his stomach on the bed, and gives a deep sigh.

'I'm meeting a deadline.'

'Yes, of course.'

He laughs in spite of himself because I said it too fast. We both wait a few seconds to see which way the conversation will go. I know Leo very well, and he knows me equally well, but we wouldn't dream of giving that game away. I'm sitting on the edge of a brown broken-down armchair; there must be about fifty million brown, broken-down armchairs like this in Europe, all broken by unhappy intelligent men. In my black coat and with my hands folded, I must look like a little Viennese governess.

Leo has been on so many sides, loved so many people and told so many variegated lies in his short lifetime, that he likes to start off nowadays with a clean slate in the case of each new or newish human being. He's afraid someone will try to hold him to some promise made in the past or re-interrogate him about a piece of behaviour. After lying on his stomach uneasily for a minute, he finds I'm not going to do this. So that instead of having to put his hands over his ears and howl out 'No!' he begins to enjoy my company. It occurs to him that my visit may have sexual implications. He looks at me and says:

'I like your coat.'

'Thanks. I like your pyjamas.'

'They are nice, aren't they? The pattern's fresh.'

'Very. I hate those modern pyjamas with a sort of sagging Judo front.'

He looks down at his stripes like a disappointed child. No sagging Judo front. Poets love modern life; Leo must have seen the Judo pyjamas advertised and wanted them. Michael once described Leo amusingly as 'a genuine man of 1969. Has had a nervous breakdown.' Actually he does look strained; he has a clear milky skin and lumps come up behind it and disrupt his face when he's unhappy. But I've seen his face smooth with happiness, both before and after his heart was broken by the screwed-up paper vocation.

I understand he must be working hard and may even be in severe mental distress, because he wants to chatter about unimportant things. I've learnt from Michael that you must *never* ask a poet whether you're interrupting his work; you always are. His thoughts are his work, and the sort of person he is. His daily conversation will tell you exactly how deeply his thinking goes; when Michael's irresponsible, haphazard and gay, I know that the thought is of the most agonising kind and on fundamental issues.

Leo says:

'I bought a new mackintosh the other day. It was absolutely transparent like a jelly-fish.' He giggles. 'It was just ironed together, you know the sort. And a sleeve came off when I was going down to Brighton on the Brighton Belle.'

'What did you do? Throw it out of the window?'

'No. I threw part of my handkerchief out of the window instead.' He makes a comical gesture from the mattress. 'But that wretched sleeve! I had to walk about in the rain with my elbow pinched in, to hold it in position. And it's very difficult not to pinch *both* in together. And when I was introduced to the head of the Brighton Technical College he immediately began to talk about second-hand clothes! So I just took the sleeve off and held it.'

'Is that it over there?'

'Yes. You can have it if you like, as a souvenir.'

'OK. I'll send it out to Michael, as the latest thing from London. But you must sign it, like a cheque.'

His face changes, and he sits up in a tub-shape, deadly serious.

'How is Michael?'

His eyes are fixed on me to drag out the essential information. He wants my answer to be *apocalyptic.* And I'm just about to give him the very answer he wants, when I'm struck by the resemblance to Zoë in one of her bolting-eye moments. She wanted the materialist's answer, and I gave it to her, and then attacked her for it. I don't want to attack Leo, so I think for a second and give him something truthful:

'He just wants some money to buy some books, you know.'

I'm instantly annoyed to see Leo getting his mystical small change out of this; he looks angelic. I tick him off:

'Don't be sloppy about Michael.'

But he's already hit an emotional storm, and his voice is choked with respect. It's absolutely sickening, far worse than Zoë. I say relentlessly:

'Slop, slop, slop.' (I know exactly how he feels; only because I feel exactly the same am I furious with him for bringing it out into the open.)

He gets up off the bed, trembling, with his eyes wet, and staggers across the room to get the mackintosh sleeve, which at any moment will turn into some gigantic symbol, a great tear-bottle from the bedrooms of poverty-stricken English poets who have kept the faith and actually know what it is. He's at it already, listen to him!

'I'm sorry, I can't help crying. It's what the clairvoyants call "a mental weeping". They can see it inside.' He's holding the sleeve and staring at it. 'It's so sad.' He's got the wretched thing tightly against his chest now. 'If I could break off a piece of myself and send it to him I would, so that he's not alone . . . There's no place for the real poets in England, and they've *driven him out!*'

I've just about had enough of a grown man in pyjamas weeping over a plastic mackintosh sleeve. Besides, every word he says is true. So I say inexorably:

'Why don't you break off the Penguin book of Italian verse and send that to him?'

'What Penguin book of Italian verse?' he says, truculent and real again. He turns around, all ready to kill me: red eyes.

'That one you're using as a spare leg to prop up the gas-ring.'

He peers at it, astonished. Then he twists his head

sideways and slowly reads out the title: 'The Pen-gwhin-Book-of –'

'So it is! Good Lord, and I've boiled all those kettles on it. You're quite right, Arabella, I've just remembered, it *is* Michael's.' He laughs over it, tears dried up like spring rain.

(Michael's actual words to me in the letter were: 'Go and see that blithering imbecile, Leo. He's not a snide careerist, he's an utter bastard. He's probably my best friend. I loathe him. He's completely trustworthy.')

Leo is crouching down, still holding his portion of mackintosh. He pulls the book out and turns over a few pages. There's silence.

'It's not very good,' he says thoughtfully, 'he can have it back. Tell him I kept it as long as I could.' This comes over his shoulder like some acid splashing up.

'Leo!'

He sniffs, having suddenly remembered he was crying a minute ago.

'Well, you were nasty to me. You get away with murder just because you're Michael's sister. You come in here all dressed up like something out of Dior –'

'Oh no. Please. Balmain.'

'Dior. And all scented up, and here am I, lying in bed with bronchitis,' he coughs healthily, 'having been swizzled out of my life by literature!'

Leo, whose moods change as fast as you can turn the knob on a radio, throws his head back and laughs hectically.

'Well, Michael's been swizzled too.'

'Yes, but I've been more swizzled.' He has a quick look

to see what effect he's having on me. None; I'm careless and just that minute looked out of the window. He says suddenly: 'I'm having a simply beastly life.'

'So am I!'

'You!'

'Yes *me*!'

'You can do anything you like.'

'So can you.'

'You've got money.'

'You've got time. And no responsibilities.'

He goes back to the centre of his bed silently with a compass and a biro, and begins to etch some message into the plastic sleeve.

'What are you writing?'

'I'm writing: "But bears it out even to the edge of doom."' His voice shakes.

'Don't put that. He'll only sneer at it.'

'He won't inside.' He goes on mumbling with self-pity as he does it. '*He's* all right. He's got away. He's changed his intelligence centre. He won't lose his arrogance now. But *I'm* still here, in the clutches of the ruthless Miss Mouse of English poetry.'

'Who is the ruthless Miss Mouse?'

'They're all mice, unless they're Judas Iscariots.'

'But why?'

'Because they don't know enough. And stupidity means cruelty.'

There's so much bitterness in his voice that my shoulders droop, and I take out my bright green patent-leather bag and look among the objects inside it for a lipstick. The contents of this bag are always strange to me, just as though it belonged to another woman. And so I take out on loan a tiny hand-mirror on a chromium rod that expands like a telescope, and a lipstick so big you could pack a bomb mechanism inside it, and with these objects provided by a stranger from another life I paint in a stranger's creamy little red mouth with a luscious lower lip. Ready!

Leo knows that I've stopped living his life. That means he doesn't have to live it either, and he instantly cheers up. He's finished scratching and says happily:

'There you are! The Penguin book of plastic verse in Pitman's shortbread. I'll just read it back to you: '*Bonjour, Hellcat, voici les lettres de mon moulin.*' He collapses all over the bed and then asks: 'Would you like some tea?'

'Yes. Love some.'

He's got a magnificent brown kettle, which has been burnt out a couple of times and in which you're allowed to boil eggs, underwear, or anything else you can think of. I don't know which of us is the better at improvisation. Leo talks to his kettle and scolds it, as I do my car. The main points of his life are his weekly visits to the Social Security office and to the launderette. At both of these social centres he has a full life. He bullies the Social Security clerks, at the launderette he sulks if he doesn't get 'his own' machine, and yet he's greatly, incomprehensibly loved for the extreme sweetness of his nature. Ask any of these people about him and they'll say with force: 'Oh, *him*,' and after a second: 'He's all right,' and still later: 'You can't help liking him.' And they'll go off smiling. Like Michael, he knows how to get the juice out of ordinary life; this extreme goodness of heart seems to go with a natural stylishness. My father can't *bear* ordinary life; a woman in a dirty cardigan with two pockets on the stomach misshapen by handkerchiefs makes him bristle up, the sight of a coarsely patterned Formica table with brown tea-cup rings on it and large yellow crumbs will cause him a temporary loss of personality, his ego buries itself in one of his shoes and leaves the rest of his body to look after itself, grey, inert. This kettle, which is giving Leo so much pleasure, would probably send him to bed and give him asthma into the bargain. And yet each of them asks, one of the inner, and the other of the outer life: 'Is this the best there is?'

Leo sings:

'Three German officers crossed the Rhine – yo-ho, yo-ho!'

He rolls his eyes, clown-like. He's ready to be unfaithful with his whole soul and *at once* to anyone who comes up in the conversation.

I name a mutal friend, just to see what happens – or perhaps because I can't bear Leo to be wasted.

'Oh he's such a lavatory-windowite!' says Leo. Or, 'Oh he's just a ramshackle seething intellectual in a green coat. He thinks with his mind, the idiot.'

And so we go on, drinking tea (which I daren't think about) and abusing everyone: 'Oh he's such a carrot. And she's a milk bottle, it's appalling. He makes his own bread, and when you go there you have to eat it. Ergot! He'll end up in the mad-house chewing leaves . . . Oh *him*, he describes a poem instead of evaluating it. He's just a short, stumpy woman with broad hips, I see him in my tea-leaves every day! *Him* – he can't grasp the smallest philosophical idea, but he'll steal your personality and woo you back with it on the same side of the disc! That's worth four hundred pounds from the Arts Council these days. Have you heard about his corset, his wig, his socks, his hot-water bottle, his carrier bag with the kippers in it? He's got all the grants, he's on all the committees, he gives orders from the lavatory seat, and it turns out his wife's got a private income. He's just a town Jew smelling a rose, so what's all this about bucolic rapture? It's got me. They've got me. I can't fight it.'

'I like your breadth and tolerance, Leo.'

Every time I laugh I feel I'm being unfaithful to someone, but that applies to ordinary life too.

'Blow your own strumpet,' says Leo affably, 'because no one else is going to blow it for you.'

'Nonsense! I spend my time blowing other people's.'

Leo has dug his spoon into a rough hole in the corner of a cardboard packet of castor sugar; he scratches busily in the blue interior like a prospector looking for something solid. He's going to tell me some merciless truth in his present open-handed mood. The fug in this room is beginning to send me to sleep; I feel too dulled to get up and go. But if I stay I'll get a dose of 'home truths' because Leo has shaken off the *deadline* apathy that kept him lolling on the bed until I arrived, and with his new wakeful strength he wants to work, and to do that he must first get rid of me.

'Yes, Arabella,' he says, giving me a full black look, 'don't you feel as though someone else has stuffed your inside and your soul into their pocket?'

This is so much what I do feel that I nod vigorously.

'*They* do it all the time, if you let them,' he says grimly.

He enlarges the cardboard hole jaggedly with his finger, and lifts out a pyramid of white sugar. He's absorbed in his own thoughts as in a newspaper. I can feel the fug anaesthetising me like a dream; I have to prop up my head since it's turned to suet. Why don't I run away? Because I want him to frighten me, to shock me into being myself by uttering some fundamental truth which will chill my ardour for my married Wolf, stiffen me, and make me hard-boiled enough to cope with life. I want the sort of fear I brought off the Moubra, which bound up all the trailing loose-ends of my personality and in one fell swoop made me independent. Although I only came for a book, I find that all the time what I really wanted were these things. And in order to get them I've let myself fall into the bottom of the armchair, dragged down by the weight of my coat, and here I lie, aggressively waiting for my spoonful of bitter sugar which will help me to live. And refusing, blankly refusing to go until I've got it. What a nasty little Viennese governess I've turned out to be!

'Arabella.'

'Yes.' I'm cautious, even sullen, afraid that he'll stop talking about me. Oh I just want one unflattering picture of myself, so that I can clench my fists and throw myself at life, and say: 'I'll show you!'

'You're looking very sweet at the bottom of my chair.'

'No I'm not.'

'Yes you *are.*' He shouts the last word at me.

We're moving away from the sort of truth I need. Shall I prompt him by describing how people impose on me and exploit me, while I run every day in the same deep rut, unfulfilled, and wondering whether there will ever be a life for me? All he has to do is to tell me what a ninny I am, what a coward. It's not much to ask. I say hopefully:

'Do you think I'm a coward?'

'You? No!'

'Oh yes I am. You don't know me.' I try to take over the conversation before it gets away from me again. 'Take my attitude to men. I'm unsuccessful because I always choose the type like my father, bright-eyed sportsmen with black eyebrows, big shoulders and experience. They're the only type I've learnt to recognise *as men.* And they bully me until I get to the point when I only know it's my duty to go to bed with someone who doesn't like me, who bullies me and criticises me.'

I've hurt his vanity, but instead of hurting mine in return he says with positive understanding:

'Oh I know that sort. They take what they need from life, and don't put anything back.'

Isn't it hopeless? That's the trouble with Leo, you don't know which way he'll turn. Any other day and he would have blasted me out of the room! Instead of that, he's human, sympathetic and affectionate. He's giving me what he gives to all his friends (and for which they're not a bit grateful), the present of a beneficial state of mind.

I start to put myself together physically. By now Leo has got used to me being there and is even enjoying it, after the grudging non-welcome on my arrival. I interrupted his thoughts, I prevented him from working, I talked about a certain type of man (not his type; he's the spiritual volcano type, a dingy Lord of the Bed-sitting-room, hopelessly corrupt, hopelessly innocent, born to look after others and to dip himself much too deeply in their affairs), and now because he wants to understand not only me but this certain type of man as well, I'm off! I start to button up the important black bosom of my coat. Yes, I'm just as selfish as everyone else. I was out for myself. I thought I could rely on him to be rude to me and to give me a jolt, but if he isn't up to it, well then, I shall hurry off at once. And get on as well as I can without it.

'Goodbye, Leo.'

'Are you going already?' He looks lost, and suddenly doesn't want to be alone with his thoughts.

'Yes. I'm late. I'll get into trouble.' This is true; there's no spare time in my life with my father, it all has to be accounted for.

I gather up the Italian book and the plastic sleeve, and swing slightly from foot to foot like a schoolgirl who wants to get away from books and fug out into the fresh air.

He lifts himself off the bed moodily. We embrace with deep affection, almost like lovers. In fact, more lovingly. His firm milk-pale face says:

'Now you take great care of yourself.' He stares into my eyes and pricks my cheeks with his.

I feel remorse. What a nice man. I hug him tenderly and kiss one shoulder of warm striped pyjama. If my own problems weren't so pressing, and my own life so empty, I'd stay and prevent him from going back to the exhausting inner toil he fears so much.

'No, it's *you*, Leo. You're the one who must take care.' I stop and ask him anxiously, as though I could do something about it: 'Will you be all right?'

'No!' says Leo with absolute conviction.

'That's all right then!'

The humour releases us both, and I can leave him. I make off down the steps, glad to have a framework of duties and housing problems to make me hurry. So much easier than returning to your own mind, like Leo. I know he must be as sick of his own emotions as I am of mine, but it's his business in life to get to know himself, day after day, and not to be paid for it, but to be ostracised, to grow grey, to keep well away from false poets and so to be at a loss for the society of his own kind, to keep away from poetry readings where everybody will be cheated, and to go on digging in his own forehead, honourably, hopefully, silently, *arrogantly*.

If you removed people like Leo from society, Zoë and my father would have to make their own values; they wouldn't know the moral price of things. The fabric of their own thoughts wouldn't hold them up. Instead they take their values (ungratefully and without even knowing it) all ready-made from a young man who lives alone with a brown kettle. And a second with a shaved head in a concrete flat near Karachi. But then literature can't live without life. And Father *is* life.

The shops always seem to be just closing when I get to them. This King Solomon's mines breath from the dry-cleaners, soap-suds from a launderette, and a throb of jazz from a record shop, are the last sighs of life from the past day. Oh, here's a delicatessen open. I go in and stare at the false vegetables stogged in mayonnaise, and wonder if I can pass them off to my father as food. Yes, with some bright conversation and an expensive soup (gluey pots, Michael!) I might do it. There's usually a lull in the nagging at this time of the year. We're both fit after skiing, and the house and furniture become just house and furniture.

There's the AC waiting for me like a dog. I look

apprehensively at the sky. There's water up there, and she can smell it. Only one drop of it has to fall on her bonnet and she coughs and won't move.

I drive like the devil to get back to Holland Park before Father. In fact I drive like a garage mechanic, and I always have done. Father likes to be welcomed; the house must be occupied. And I'm always afraid he'll say again: 'Get a housekeeper if you can't manage. We can afford it.' I imagine an efficient middle-aged woman with no nerves moving in, marrying Father, and prising me off my rock, away from my little velvet bedside chair, flickering lamp and rosewood chest of drawers, and my window with the view of the lawn and two apple trees. With a fish-slice and a tin-opener, she'd have no difficulty at all in getting rid of me. Once adrift in the ocean, I should quickly lose heart and die. Even the curious relationship I have with this machine I'm driving, even that reassures me of my identity at the moment. It's a form of talking to oneself. There's the crack in the exhaust pipe which gives the car a magnificent low road-moan, like a trump of dust. A scorching purple haze flows out of it, which is forbidden. I know all the slow lanes of traffic, all the slow traffic lights in west and north-west London. It seems to me now as I race down towards Marble Arch (before turning right) that the light is brighter in the centre of the city and the people more avid and neatly dressed – and, as though to control this, there are road-signs of greater severity with stronger colours.

Somewhere down here among these roads with yellow warning stripes painted on them like wasps and tigers, I'm to have tea with my Wolf the day after tomorrow. Due to the Swiss holiday, it's nearly a month since our last meeting. Is this all I've been able to gain for myself on emotional terms – after flying to Switzerland, skiing all day, and driving around London in a temperamental female car – the half attentions of a twilit married wolf with a light voice?

I can't help laughing at this ludicrous score in the mathematics of having a life. And I comfort myself with a joke: 'You don't suppose there's time in a lifetime to have a life, do you? Certainly not!'

5

A dinner party for eight this evening. All friends of Father's. The men will be well dressed, important and extroverted, and the women capable and full of character, with solid healthy bodies, varnished hair and good manners. I'm not really the equal of these women because each of them has secured for herself a successful modern man, bound him to her, made herself indispensable to his life and thoughts and countered his neurosis with a pretty female neurosis of her own which she plays like a piano; she hasn't given him time to think. Because to think is to want something else. Each of them has to be, at least, a bitch, and psychologically self-sufficient, attentive to herself, otherwise she would die of boredom, since she is always doing what he wants. You can pick out the ones whose psychology isn't equal to the job, the women who come off those abysmal jet flights with tight lips; when they get to a stuffy hotel lounge they recline mud-pale with tiredness – while the wise ones, the bitches, go straight to the bar, order an interesting drink, and start to make a list of their wants before their husbands can get in with a list of theirs. There's nothing a rich, discontented husband likes better than satisfying wants. It fills his soul to the brim.

No, I haven't caught myself such a man. And the security of these women, with their heavy ropes of glowing white pearls, their terracotta necks, their smart shoes with buckles on them, and the ordinary events which they seem to have time for, interests me like good weather with pearl-white clouds sailing along in clear skies.

The food has all arrived and been unpacked. The butler and cook will be here at five-thirty. The table was laid with freshly polished silver by the cleaner this morning. The flowers look reasonable and it's really too warm for a fire – I can see the birds in the back garden carrying twigs up to some nest they've rigged up under the eaves. Father likes to be kept up to date on any livestock that appears in his garden; like the people he employs, he wants to know down to the last decimal point whether they're justifying their keep. When I told him in the cold weather that I'd put out some bread for the birds, he thought carefully and then said they must have a mixed diet, with fat in it. The point is that they're his birds, and naturally he wants them properly fed. They must cheep at the right times and lay eggs at the correct seasons in well-cared-for nests. I laughed at him, and he made his 'little boy' face. The extraordinary thing about Father is that he can always find some additional task in a house, even when it's near perfect. I take him into the sitting-room when it's shimmering with polish, and he says without a pause to look round: 'Have you washed the jade?' The jade. Eight pieces on the oak chest. We've never in our lives washed the jade. Dusted it, yes. No, I haven't washed the jade, my dearest father, I used that unit of time (I think) to press my forehead into a door on the landing and think hungrily and in the most perfect detail you can imagine about the body of my Wolf. Did I earn the time? No; I took it and squandered it.

And now I'm going to use more jade-washing time, because I want to dance. I always dance in the sitting-room when I'm sad or bored or frustrated. This is one of the advantages of not having servants who live in. I dance modern-style on the same spot, or change to ordinary ballet. With all the curtains drawn, flushed and happy in the semi-dark, I act out my thoughts and to my astonishment I find them joyful; I have no inhibitions, not one. Sooner or later I'm going to give three or four enormous jumps across the room. I know I'm smiling as I do it (can't help it), and I know it's reasonably well done, not coarse. There is no way of describing the triumph and abandon of dancing well alone. You're so proud of your body. To your surprise you find it'll do anything, bend, quiver, glide about. As I warm up, more and more clothes come off; finally I'm down to a very short petticoat, bought at Harrods, made of slippery white material with a two-inch band of lace around the bottom, vulgar as all underwear should be. In this I fly about the room, gently but never timidly, past the old thoughts on the oak chest, the unwashed jade, the tiny green chairs which were my mother's. I play short pop records, new ones with no memories embedded in them. They're flimsy little objects at eight-and-six each, and you wouldn't think them capable of barking, chugging, growling and screaming rhythmically at the tops of their voices as they do. With each of them goes some 'lyric' – a flighty message of about twenty words which must be as spontaneous as though it had been scribbled down in a taxi rushing across London from Claridge's to the Savoy, just after dark when the city's dusty crust of cafés is alight.

Occasionally I play the two records Michael and I made in the record booth on Victoria Station. One is called '*The Nagging, Grumbling and Complaining Record*' which we made after he was sent down; and the other is '*Silence*' in which we both held our breath and the only noise is an occasional train announcement which got into the booth from the loud-speakers. Michael was to play '*Silence*' in his Notting Hill Gate room when the noise from the other tenants prevented him from working.

'Father! So early. I didn't hear you come in.'

I'm caught, almost in mid-air, half-dressed, with the whole room pounding away. I'm apprehensive, but he's friendly.

'What's all this?' He kisses me, and then looks me over, puts his arm around me for a minute and walks me to and fro like a doll. 'Dancing, is it?' He's delighted to think I'm able to amuse myself by doing graceful movements dressed only in a skimpy bit of underwear. He releases me after this curiously lengthy embrace, and sits down. He's still got his stitched soft leather gloves on, and says affably:

'Go ahead. Don't let me stop you. I'm going to look at some papers for ten minutes.' He pretends to bend over his despatch case and go seeking inside it. The record cuts itself off, and I go to it absently and put on the lightest thing I have, Peter Sarstedt. Father seems to be correcting something, but he still has his gloves on, and is too assiduous. He keeps his eyes lowered to encourage me. I stand there, defensive, on bare feet. I know that it's my task to demonstrate my innocence; after all, I used to be his 'little girl'. But I'm not innocent, Father. I'm sensuous with high sensual standards, just as you are. And any movements I make will tell you that – unless I turn it into a parody of sensuality, like those excruciating flamenco dancers. When I was alone, of course, I was completely innocent. But since you entered the room, I know myself, and really daren't make a gesture!

I perform a few inhibited movements. I can see from the stiff way Father is holding his head that he's enjoying it. I suddenly feel a gust of love for him as he sits there, meekly correcting papers in his gloves. So I do my dance, keeping the old euphoria out of my limbs, but decently pacing out a few figures, stretching my arms in pleasant oval shapes like one of Canova's sexless sculptures, and passing by him inoffensively. I even begin to enjoy it on its own terms, this new dance with all the wildness bred out of it. When it's over I flop down and we smile and look one another in the eye.

'Very good, Pigeon,' he says. 'You're nice and light on your feet.'

So he's been assessing the merits of my dance all the time!

He promptly closes the folder of papers, and says:

'Now about tonight. Have you arranged the seating?'

'Yes, all done. Eric Bennett will have his back to the radiator, does that matter?'

'No. I'd rather he complained of heat than cold when he comes here.'

'What shall I talk to him about?'

'Horses. He breeds them.'

'Shall I tell him the story about Rastras jumping over my pram when I was a baby?'

'Yes, tell him that.'

'And about me getting pink-eye?'

'You never had pink-eye. That reminds me, what's his wife's christian name? Is it Muriel? Or Brenda. It's something indeterminate like that.'

'Monica?'

'No, no it's more sweet-shop in Taunton . . .'

'Sheila, or Shei-lagh with a hard "g".' I play with him.

'No, certainly not. That's a female convict. I've got a feeling it's Marion.'

'A bit old. Marions are usually over fifty these days.'

'So am I,' says Father, amused and without malice.

'I've put on that big white damask cloth that goes nearly to the ground, because people talk much better when their legs are hidden. Honestly, Father, if you just have a polished table top they skid about with their knives and forks and feel insecure. They feel it's less of an *occasion*.'

Father loves information of this sort from me, which he feels to be a genuine initiative towards social well-being.

'Ah-ha.' He ponders it. 'Where are you putting Buffy?'

Buffy is a socialist MP and a completely unmarriageable bachelor. He's unmarriageable because he's a know-all. The only place he can get rid of all the useless information he's acquired is at a dinner party, when he corrects people throughout. Originally we thought he was such a menace that Father asked him only as a 'safe' man for me; but the mysterious result of his boorishness was that afterwards people asked who was that 'nice' man? i.e. the man who patronised and insulted them. So the moral is that you can't correct people often enough, and the more you put them in their places, the happier they are. The only man who ever silenced Buffy was Leo Johnson. He came looking for Michael once with a carrier bag of books in one hand and a packet of Weetabix in the other, and was so wrapped up in non-communication with the mice and Judas Iscariots of the outer world that he didn't even notice Buffy was in the room. Directly he'd gone, Buffy asked who was that 'nice' man? So there's a place on the treadmill for everyone.

'Next to Mrs Derriman. She's a good listener and she'll mop it all up.'

'He never bothers to talk to women like that. We need Leo or a duchess.'

'It's the same thing.'

'And Lady Escott?'

'On the other side of Eric Bennett. Next to Des Derriman. She's a bit actressy. I do hope she doesn't wear a caftan.'

'I hope she *does*. And right down to the ground. Last time she had muddy shoes.'

Oh how unforgivable of her, my eyes say to Father. He insinuates a whole world of muddy shoes and bad organisation which can only be covered by a floor-length caftan. I see Lady Escott muddying out to the bird-table in her garden for a quick snack before coming out to dine with Father. Luckily she doesn't have far to come, and probably walks here, and does heaven knows what else on the way, which is a very simple explanation for the dirty shoes and the good complexion. I say:

'She's got a good complexion, so they won't look down, Father.'

'Won't they just! You don't know Eric Bennett. The first thing he notices about a woman is her shoes.'

'Well then, he's a fetishist, and lucky to get asked out at all.'

'As one of the richest men in London I hardly think so,' says Father drily.

There's a piercing note from the front door. We're startled at our private conversation like Coppelia the doll and her magician; I've been 'cooling off' on one of the green chairs with my limbs spread out to air, and Father has been collapsed with his papers on top of him, a posture of near-abandon for him. He rises hastily.

'You can't go like that. I suppose I'll have to.'

'It's only a quarter to five, can't be the butler and co. yet.'

I wrap my dressing-gown around me, and spread a fan of magazines to cover my other clothes. I can hear that Father has opened the door and there seems to be some sort of commotion going on. It's raining outside, and simultaneously as drops strike the windows sideways the sitting-room door is butted open and in comes a huge brown dog, all wet, plodding about with soggy paws and wagging a strong brown tail recently dipped in mud. It's as though some benign nature god is paying Father out for the Lady Escott shoe-talk. In my undressed state, with only a thin house-gown on, I shrink back, and anyway I'm terrified at the size of it, as big as a lion, with no one to control it. It comes straight up to me, and I shriek. Father puts his head around the door.

'It's a greetings telegram for you.'

He's holding one of those paper envelopes splashed with Post Office gold. I daren't go up to him to take it because of the dog, which is methodically plodding around me and has just knocked over a piece of jade with its tail. And there goes a jug of flowers!

'Father, please do something about this dog!'

His head disappears, and there's some more conversation before he re-enters the sitting-room and tries to shoo the dog out. It's monstrously friendly, pats Father with its great big paws and goes on promenading.

'Father, for God's sake!' I'm laughing and on the point of shrieking again, due to the unexpectedness, the total absurdity of this large brown body thumping about.

'It doesn't seem to want to go out,' says my father.

'That's putting it mildly!'

'Is this your dog?' he calls sternly to some messenger boy who presumably is standing outside. There's a lumbering sound like someone large learning to walk.

The next instant there's a second enormous figure in the room. This one's more or less human, at least it's upright and is dressed in blue serge, army boots, a black crash-helmet and goggles, and is decorated all over with beads of water. He seems to be dumb.

'Well, is it yours?' asks Father, really exasperated.

'No . . .' He doesn't seem too sure.

'Well, what's it doing here?'

No answer. I believe the goggles make them deaf and dumb. He seems to breathe in a retarded fashion through his mouth.

'Well, please help me to get it out!'

Evidently there was a double misunderstanding. On opening the front door, Father beheld a messenger, possibly even a police messenger, together with his dog. The dog promptly entered the house like a well-trained police dog looking for cannabis resin. Father, knowing he had no cannabis resin (Michael out of the country) and unwilling to thwart authority, didn't stop it. The messenger on his side must have arrived at the door accompanied by what he took to be our dog, which naturally enough went in as soon as the door was opened.

As a consequence of this I have two soaking wet animals scuffling about on the pale carpets, knocking things over and doing enough damage to keep Eric Bennett's eyes away from Lady Escott's shoes forever. There's mud everywhere. I've never seen so much. There's more in here than there is in the garden. Actually, the GPO messenger doesn't want to give his services, you can see that from the impotence of his gestures, which the dog seems in fact to enjoy. (Thirty-love. Dog to serve.) As for Father, he's inclined to stay out of reach since he wants to wear the suit he has on this evening. Between the two of them the dog more or less does as it likes, and finally exits. I rather wish I'd put on a record for them while they amused themselves.

I'm weakened by laughter and by my vulnerability due to my near-nakedness. But a sight of Father's eyes – they're like boiling ink – stops all that.

'There's your telegram,' he says pointedly, and crams it into the pocket of my gown with some roughness 'And why aren't you changed?'

He's gone to get a dustpan and brush, and calls back:

'Go on. Upstairs. I'll clear up the mess, as usual.'

I bite my lip. Here come the bad times again.

Back to thirteen years of age, I tear upstairs. I'm in the wrong again, as I always was. I'm not giving good value.

My dress, clean underwear and stockings, rings, scent, were laid out on the bed this morning when the cleaner came. The dress is an old Mary Quant in orange paper taffeta with a very low bodice, just a ledge like the ones you use to display Grade A porcelain, and a huge longish skirt. I tried it on for Father and he approved it: 'That's right, not too smart or you'll frighten the wives. Doesn't matter how low the bosom is, cut it down if you like, but I can't have a short skirt. One of last year's dresses, is it? That's ideal. You don't want to be up to the minute, it's fast. Yes, the orange is fine against your skin.'

I tear the telegram open and gulp down the magic cypher. It's from my Wolf. He *insists* on dinner. I cram it into a drawer of underwear.

Have I got time to put my hair up? My hair's so dark that it gives me a white face when it hangs loose. After the flush of exercise, followed by the dog-opera and Father's rage, it's whiter than white at the moment. It takes fifteen minutes of careful labour to put the hair up, and then I have to stick huge black pins into it, like croquet hoops; they're painful. On top of this goes the hairpiece of black braids, it's my own hair, cut off when I left school. Fastened with a comb with sharp teeth and more croquet hoops, this structure is weighty. The difficulty is that the tone of Father's voice makes my hands tremble as though I've got Parkinson's disease. And to make a good job of an Eiffel Tower on your head you must have steady hands and an instinctive sense of your own style; there's a good deal of decision-making as you go along in such work, and your fingers must carry it out *on the spot* because hair is such slippery stuff. There's a point on either side of my head where the ends of the braids must curl under; if I get it wrong, the Tower turns into a Bun or Earphone, and the first person to notice that it's not high style is poor Father!

I've just finished this labour when the bell screams again, and I know it's the butler and cook. Hot consommé; *salade Niçoise,* she's only got to put that together; the fish is all ready; *filet en croûte*, everything laid out again, it's only a matter of good timing. A wonderfully reassuring bourgeois menu.

I let them in and show them where to put their things. My dress makes an expensive frou-frou noise like rustling pound-notes; it wasn't expensive so there's no need for them to be quelled by the sound. I have to make a pretence of knowing everything: the surprising thing is that you find the knowledge is hidden inside you. He's very fair and slow with moist porter's hands. She's not so fair but equally slow; she has no overall, apron etc. and her hair trails forward. A bad omen. In the kitchen I show her the luscious slab of *filet*; here's the marble block, as pale and mottled as a thigh, where I roll pastry to keep it cool. She looks at the meat, bewildered, and wrinkles her forehead, which is covered with pink make-up:

'Oh, but I can't do this sort of cooking!'

'Can't you cook then?'

'Yes. Just plain cooking.'

'But this *is* plain cooking. Everything's very simple. If you don't know the dish, just follow the recipe, you've got plenty of time.'

'Oh, I couldn't.' More wrinkles, of the stubborn kind.

'But you've come to us as a *cook* for the evening! I told the agency exactly what the menu was.'

'They just said a little cooking and help around, and so on.'

My heart starts to accelerate. I've got eight exacting people with wide bodies to feed, and no cook. She's obviously not up to it. Look at the way she's staring at the rolling pin, as though bewitched! To calm her down I set her to organising the olives, onions, and pistachio nuts for the drinks. She starts to drop things and needs reassuring. I do my calculations with a biro on the margin of the newspaper spread over the kitchen table. Forty minutes, and warm the oven first. Now if I do the *filet* myself and get it into the oven just before everyone arrives . . . I get an inner trembling as I hastily reorganise my activities, unable to estimate Father's goodwill and afraid it may already have flown out of the window. My nerves must be able to control his: I freeze them with fear and re-enter the sitting-room.

He's got his back to me and is lugubriously pouring a drink. I go up to him, gay and calm. He points his face towards the kitchen and makes a question out of it.

'Yes, fine!' (She can't cook, and he's so slow and careful he's bound to break something good.)

Father goes over some past dinner parties rapidly in his mind, and hits on a bad experience. He says at once:

'Make sure the meat is *hot* when it comes in. I don't want a layer of mutton fat left on my tongue. It's highly disagreeable.'

I'm dumb. There's nothing from either a sheep or a lamb on the menu tonight, and he knows it. This is one of his provocative remarks; although they are wholly illogical in context, they spring from a mental picture so strong that you must treat them respectfully. I know that the mutton fat in Father's mind is as real as the deadline in Leo Johnson's. So I throw off my dumbness and say what's necessary:

'It'll be red-hot, in that great covered silver dish, the vulgar one. I dare you to touch it with your naked hand!'

He relaxes at once, cured; you can see the neurotic bank of muscles across his shoulders subside. He swirls the coloured drink around in his glass so that the ice hits the side, and as it chimes he smiles on me apologetically.

'I know I'm silly.'

His glance drifts off down to his nails and from there to the object which made them dirty, the carpet. There are dull smudges on it. The mud-splashed glass doors into the hall have been clumsily wiped over at the bottom. I've learnt from Father that if you can seize the psychological advantage by anticipating a criticism, your opponent can never regain it. I could turn the tables on Father by an exclamation made to sound natural: 'Oh, you've left them patchy.' But the mud accompanied the telegram, *my* telegram; in that case I might lose the exchange after the opening shot. So I wait until he bends over absent-mindedly and drops the ash of his cigar into a little jade bowl.

'Father!'

He starts guiltily. I say:

'Jade too!' (It's so transparent that if Michael were here he would have laughed out loud and ruined everything.)

He almost makes a move as though he's going to empty it, but quickly recovers himself and says:

'Oh, they'll soon be full up if I know Des.'

I decide to return to the pandemonium in the kitchen while I'm still winning. Father has begun to equalise, and since his heart is in the game and mine isn't, I can't waste my strength, especially when mine is the strength of anxiety.

In the kitchen, which is already steamed up, the first thing I see is the cook's hysterical face. She is building and then taking apart a *salade Niçoise* like a child with a construction toy and hours to play with it. The butler has caught the panic and slowed himself down in order to deal with it; he is attentively reading the labels on the bottles which have been put out for him. In the ordinary way I'd snap out a request for some champagne cocktails, but going up to him as to another little child, I put the suggestion to him in a low voice. He seems partially to hear me, and answers with a thoughtful nod. I take over the *salade Niçoise* and put the cook to *sauté* potatoes and garden peas. There is a good green salad to be made. I squint at her to see whether she's capable of washing a lettuce. I can hear another sound from far away in the sitting-room. Father is having one of his conversations with me; these follow a familiar pattern. He goes into another room and talks to himself. Months later it'll turn out that he was reminding me to renew the licence for my car.

The front-door bell again. Isn't someone ridiculously early? The butler plods off interested, just like the dog butting doors open: still, I'm impressed to see him respond at all.

I'm working ruthlessly and fast at the big kitchen table – it's the old-fashioned kind with a wooden top (covered with layers of newspaper which I tear off as I go), which has been scrubbed so often it's got a white soapy patina like institution flesh. My cook asks for a wire container in which to shake the lettuce dry; she's determined to show me that she's used to doing things the *right* way, implying that in this house things are done the wrong way. If she only knew how little it mattered to me personally. And in addition, years of handling Father have given me the edge in situations of this sort. I say horribly:

'We always shake each leaf separately by hand. Otherwise the salad is wet in the middle.'

The butler returns, having summoned Father to the door, something he loathes when he's busy. Who was it? Some employee of Father's. But from where, from the office? He doesn't think so. At the same time, I can hear the telephone ringing and Father will never answer that. I go to it, leaving my lettuce-leaf shaker and reader of wine labels hard at work, shaking and reading.

'Fifteen minutes late? Quite all right. Yes, just past Notting Hill Gate.'

I put the phone down with my kitchen hand and behold Father in conversation with Mr Chorny, our Hungarian road-sweeper. This old man has some complaint which keeps him bent double; he was supplied with an expensive £50 steel corset on the National Health to keep him upright but discarded it instantaneously, of course. He has a little Borough Council barrow with brushes stuck into it which he wheels about, and his circular posture fits itself comfortably against the rail of it, so that the two go together, barrow and circle. He's indefatigable in his sweeping, to and fro and up and down, never a spare minute; he even sweeps out the short driveway up to Father's house and makes sure the iron gates ride easily on their hinges. I believe this behaviour is something to do with Father's local prestige. Father always gives the appearance of employing people when he talks to them, and some people are so duped by this that they actually imagine they *are* employed by him. They salute him and give him scraps of information. In the end all edges become blurred; Father assumes certain people are on his payroll and issues streams of orders and instructions; they, on receiving the instructions, assume he must be right because such a man cannot be wrong. These arrangements bring happiness to both sides, since they give the lost Mr Chorny the right to ring our doorbell, attracted as he is by activity and the arrival of unknown personages. It's perfectly true to say that whenever you give a party, however small, there will be more unnecessary telephone calls, wrong numbers, and rings at the doorbell from the Mr Chornys of the world, than at any other time.

I haven't time to make the pastry. But by luck and foresight, there's some frozen pastry in the deep freeze. Four packets; just enough if I'm clever with my hands which won't stop trembling – rather like my Wolf's.

6

Here come the actors! It's Buffy first. A second ago I closed the oven door on my perfected *filet en croûte*, glazed all over with egg, and my face and neck are still glowing from the hot gassy breath of it; and with relief. I even had enough nervous strength to make four-pronged patterns in the white pastry with a fork. Now I'm posed by the fireplace, only the redness, and the fact that my hands throb with veins, could give me away. Father has put out a photograph of Michael! It's on the davenport which everyone has to pass as they enter the room. I'm incredulous, but there it is; Michael is reading in a deck-chair in the shady, leafy monochrome photograph's world, the nose and mouth are sullen and beautiful, so like Father's really, when he's just made up his mind. (Is this an effort to *include* Michael?)

'Hullo, Buffy. The best organised man in London is first.'

'I could smell something cooking.'

'I hope not. Oh, I like that sash.'

Buffy is wearing a fancy shirt and a scarlet sash with a thick fringe. With his bright ginger hair and sideburns, it's rather a shock and makes him more unmarriageable than ever. He's very, very tall and I try to make him sit down as soon as possible. I look at him to see whether he's going to bother to talk to me but he's already watching the door avidly – if only he were looking for women! But I know that blood-thirsty glare, he's hoping for a man of principle he can correct both fundamentally and in detail. Wrong house, Buffy! Thank God no one discusses education at Father's dinner parties.

Here's Lady Escott – same old caftan! Father's face makes a diabolical 'I told you so!' right behind her head. His daring takes my breath away, but I suppose she's only a woman in his view, and also he's not involved with her in any stockbroking enterprise. So if she turned and caught him at it, it wouldn't be the end of his world. I'm disturbed by my rapid exposure of motive in these terms – is it because I talk with Father's language and think with his thoughts? I believe it is.

Mrs Derriman, my favourite; with a gentle nature, she remains pink and pretty, and my spirits rise at the sight of her. There's powder on the white hair on either side of her face. Derriman is like a great mahogany wardrobe crammed into a lounge suit, all bulky angles, and a pair of cupboard doors with mirrors on them liable to burst open down the front, but his style shows like Father's in his narrow shoes and up at the top there's a tiny orchid in his lapel. His face is of sliced beef, and his voice low and rumbling with so much gravy in it that it makes you want to clear your throat. I start clearing mine as he comes in.

Buffy has seen the orchid, and shows signs of life. Any moment now he'll break into words. I don't like the rate he drinks his champagne cocktail, as though he's already decided he's going to be bored and is determined to make his own entertainment.

Ah, Eric Bennett, the shoe-spotter, a real dandy. He takes over the conversation on the spot, and pacing about the pale drawing-room goes up to each of us with a bright comment and makes us ginger ourselves up and enjoy life a little bit more than we really want to. I suppose he's acquired the habit from checking over his horses. His eyes are so bright, as though they've just been washed and waxed. By contrast his wife has dull, sexy eyes, and a way of hanging her hands from the wrist as though she was drip-drying them. She's always very well dressed in clothes that don't suit her. In no time Eric's pranced up to the photograph of Michael (now I understand why he's always one up on Father) and has said:

'I haven't seen a photograph of someone in a garden *for years*. It takes me back. Do you remember the time when everything important seemed to happen on lawns, under trees? And now –'

'Oh now it all goes on in Czechoslovakia,' says Buffy loudly.

Lady Escott wastes everybody's time by laughing at this. And I wonder why, until I realise suddenly that she finds Buffy attractive. I look at him with new eyes; he's worse than ever.

Meanwhile Father has strolled up to gaze at the photograph with Eric Bennett. He's completely at ease, so much so that I guess he must be very tense. With his voice full of affection he says:

'It's good of Michael, isn't it? I took it last summer Before he . . . went off.'

I open my mouth in astonishment, because I took the photograph myself. Not that it matters at all who took it. But it creates goodwill for Father, of course, and gives an entirely false picture of a relationship in which a loving, tolerant father continues to cherish his son, photograph him, and include him in the conversation, a son who merely 'went off', a fact which the father lets fall reluctantly, in an aside, and wishing he had not begun a sentence that way, a way that forced him to conclude it with a truth which was painful to him.

Now that I know the conversation is going to be of Michael for the next few minutes, I quickly rehearse the answers Father will expect me to give. I must represent Michael as an astute member of the python-skin set, working under cover for Christie's, buying up jade. India and Pakistan must appear to be logical extensions of Oxford and Mayfair, territories which Michael has annexed for amusing, commercial reasons. And there, smart and carefree, he lives it up, making large sums of money without effort from both commercial television and occasional scoops as a jade merchant, and hasn't the slightest intention of coming back to boring old England after the life he's used to out there. As it happens, only yesterday when I wrote to Michael, Father said to me: 'Did you ask him about the jade?' He very much wants Michael to add to his collection, and asks me regularly about this. He even suggested he might send us some Persian caviar. I haven't yet passed his messages on, knowing perfectly well that Michael's struggles out there alone in the heat have nothing to do with such matters, which would simply enrage him.

Eric Bennett is fully prepared to feed my father the question he seems to need. He asks:

'What's he up to in Pakistan? I bet he's having the best of it out there.'

He looks cheerfully at Father, whose face at once changes to one of thought and gravity.

'Between you and me, I think . . .' Father hesitates and looks at Eric Bennett to see whether he's worthy of such a confidential matter, and then takes the plunge and decides to trust him. 'I think he's gone for some religious experience. I know he wants to work for famine relief as well. The two things tie in together.' He looks away into the near-distance for a second without focussing, like a holy man, and then goes on: 'I rather admire the young people of today, you know, Eric. They put their philosophy into practice, and achieve some very remarkable things.' This stylish finish is supported by the full beam of Father's regard, centred directly from under those black arches into the full beam of Eric Bennett's. It's like two cars with their headlights full on facing one another, not forgetting that each has a tankful of champagne.

'I agree,' he says forcefully. I know he's taken by surprise by this artful *volte-face* of Father's because he's busy rearranging the muscles of his face to suit the new emotional content of the conversation. It's like a woman suddenly shaping up the cushions on her sofa so as to make them look respectable for a visiting priest, after they've been crushed into improper shapes by her lover.

'I absolutely agree,' says Eric again. 'One can't help respecting them. And I wish Michael the very best of luck in whatever he puts his hand to. I know he'll make a success of it.'

I've never seen two happier-looking middle-aged men. Eric is glowing radiantly with the trust that Father has just put in him, and has found things in his own heart that more than match it. Father is glowing at having done the trusting, in picking a wealthy business associate who can appreciate his son on unworldly terms, and thus rousing both of them up to a new moral esteem for one another. There's a feeling of well-being all round, and Father says apologetically to Eric:

'I haven't any up-to-date news, I'm afraid. But he writes to Arabella.' He smiles rather brokenly at me.

Everyone looks towards me, and there's a special interval for me to make my contribution to the good atmosphere with a little real news. After all, poor Father can't do that, because Michael doesn't write to him!

'Oh, just scrappy notes.' (I had a five-page letter only this morning.) 'He seems to spend most of the time on the beach.'

'On the *beach* . . . ?'

'He says it's the coolest place.'

'He's got to have *some* relaxation, after all,' says Father, warning me that if I damage Michael's integrity, I damage his.

'He's just an old slacker,' I say perversely. 'Same old Michael, can't settle to anything for long.' What makes me say this? It's something to do with their well-fed faces.

'I don't believe that for a minute,' says Eric so warmly that Father gives him a sharp look.

'He's got a butterfly mind.' I've simply got to run Michael down, in a sense in order to keep him clean. 'He goes mad about something, and then just drops it.' Have I gone far enough? I look around at the uneasy faces. I'm searching for one last provocative sentence with which to protect my beloved Michael. I'm taking away the warm feelings they had for the Michael who was praying and feeding the hungry; I'm taking away their guilt. 'I think he just went for some party, and he'll come back when it's over.'

Buffy laughs so noisily it's like a shout and makes you want to leave the room.

'And a very good reason for going anywhere!' He always makes a gigantic effort towards smartness in this way; his basic apprehension of what is smart isn't bad, but it's the clumping way he expresses it which is so dismal. It's always a bit off. Naturally Lady Escott laughs scattily. I see what Father means about those shoes.

This disagreeable laughing-duet has ruined the atmosphere of decent, almost noble, sentiment, so carefully mixed by my father, who likes to talk until he gets the emotional temperature in the house just right. It's my fault, of course, for introducing superficialities. But Father put out the photograph as an extension of his own personality, part of his empire, which would gain for him yet another layer of identity – he must know that it would make Michael throw up to be shown off as a pious little do-gooder. The whole thing is nauseating. As we go in to dinner, Father puts this sentence into my ear:

'Do you always have to have all the attention for yourself?'

It goes on stinging inside my head for the rest of the meal.

My God, how slow the butler is. My consommé is only tepid. Actually I loathe it with sherry in it, it always tastes as though it's gone bad. Des Derriman drinks his eagerly as though it's blood. Thank heavens Eric Bennett is entertaining Father and striking just the right decent note too:

'... in the middle of Piccadilly Circus the cabby suddenly got out and slammed the door. Next minute I saw him right over on the other side of the road with a blind man, took him across six lanes of traffic, then had to wait while the traffic went by, then back into the cab and drove on without a word. I don't think there's much wrong with this country.'

Father looks pleased as though somehow this reflects well on Michael, who's presumably doing the same sort of thing in Pakistan.

'It's a great country,' says Des Derriman. 'Although the power of the Church has been broken, and many of the old establishments, the fundamental values are there all right, inside the ordinary man in the street.'

He butters up a piece of French bread and sends it down to his wardrobe.

Father nods, and recalls that he stumbled on the same fundamental values in himself only the other day.

'I was surprised,' he admits it about himself, 'there was a film on I knew Arabella wanted to see, and, as it happened, I wanted to see it myself. But there was just this old ingrained notion that one shouldn't go to the cinema on a Sunday afternoon, and I'm afraid I couldn't go against it, somehow, even though I wanted to.'

Everyone nods again respectfully, glad to think that in business and in the home there are things that Father can't go against. It's good to think that this very beautiful dining-room with some excellent oils by English masters – a white horse by Stubbs, an interior of Lintz cathedral by Heyden, no nudes, only decent horses and cathedrals – it's good to think they were all obtained by a man who wouldn't go to the cinema on Sunday afternoon.

The curious fact is that none of the women present seems to be in the least bit moved by the extremely decent feelings of her husband. Even pink Mrs Derriman, although she nodded with the rest of them, has a curious look in her eye. I have noticed though that one or two of the very, very rich widows of such men tend to come up with stories like this late in life, in which they, too, have decent feelings. But wives, never.

How I admire these women and envy them their safety! They've done the right things at the right moments in life, and ended up in Father's beautiful amber dining-room as their reward. Whereas I, with my bad French and my inability to capture the right sort of man, am here only by my father's courtesy and not as part of a real life. I'm always living by proxy on the edge of someone else's life, just tagging along.

Mrs Derriman and Mrs Bennett describe amusing things their husbands have done recently, sometimes quite intimate things that took place in a bedroom, or else it's an airport story. These are the only places where they're up against the rough facts of life, for they have ex-directory telephone numbers and chauffeurs to park their cars. All the major irritations of life have been dealt with long ago.

The husbands listen peacefully to these stories, laughing heartily at their own behaviour and admitting to quite serious weaknesses. As the wives go on talking they rid themselves of certain grudges against their husbands by hinting that they're not 'allowed' to do certain things and that their time is very strictly controlled, and that they have no money of their own and no self-confidence because their husbands are always criticising them: 'And Eric said about my mink, "What, that old bit of Belsize cat?"' After the sherry and white wine, these stories are leaked out like those of Russian literary men in detention, and a tale of frustration, frost-bite, and harassment emerges. These grudges push their way to the surface against the will of the talkers. The husbands bear it all, laughing or plaintively interceding for themselves, but on the whole putting a very good face on it. Much better actors with much better roles to play in life, they have to cope with more difficult scenes than these any day of their lives. They merely wait expansively until it's over, and then go on talking as though nothing had happened. If they end up as better psychologists it's only because they're much more determined to get their own way. Buffy is now the only man at the table whose bedroom habits haven't been described publicly, and he seems to resent it and starts talking about them himself.

'When I was travelling around Eastern Europe with my father we often had to share the same bedroom, and he'd always get to sleep *first* and immediately start snoring.'

'Don't!' comes out of the caftan.

'I used to get desperate. In the end I'd simply have to wake him up so that we could start even.'

'Buffy, how mean.'

'It didn't work. He'd be drifting off straight away, and I'd be left behind again on the seashore with the sea going out. It was hell.'

At that moment in comes the *filet en croûte*, it's uncovered and is shown to be as golden brown as a Roman brick ruin and a thing of great beauty. Father's eyes light up. Pastry! His delight is so ingenuous that I could go up and kiss him. I'm touched by the simplicity of these men around the table (with the exception of Buffy, of course) and by their efforts to make life work. They're emotional men, they like one another, and try like hell to enjoy life and to find good things inside themselves. Alternatively, if they can't find good things they don't go on searching as Michael would, but manage perfectly well without them. Hooray! The sun comes out and a brass band seems to be playing in the dining-room. The table shimmers and clinks. People talk more loudly at the sight of the meat, they purr, laugh, and cough, and because of this I can only just hear the telephone ringing far away in the distance. My cook certainly won't go to it, she told me quite plainly that she wouldn't go further than the kitchen passage, too busy at the stove, checking the controls etc.

As I go to the telephone I realise that I've hardly had a morsel to eat, and that I'm dead tired, scarlet in the face, and shall be up until at least two o'clock in the morning. Why, I've spent ten years now giving such dinner parties to build up Father's prestige while my own desires, and especially my friends, have all been lost on the way. I think this was the reason I didn't want Father to gain himself *even more* identity from Michael's photograph this evening. And especially a form of identity which he hadn't earned.

'Oh Leo, it's you.' A friend! Or is he? You can never be sure with Leo.

'Arabella, did you know it was bright moonlight outside?'

'Moonlight!' It's a word from another world of light lawless, transparent, vivid evenings. I've seen Leo just sniffing the streets because he says they smell so good. And Michael says the streets of London make the most beautiful moonlight in the world.

'The brightest, whitest moonlight you ever saw. And it's all *free* in the streets. And we're going to go out and dance in it, Arabella.'

'Are we?' I suddenly feel I'm loved and wanted.

'Yes. Straight away!'

The butler's passing and I just have time to ask him, 'Have you taken the vegetables round for the second time?' I return to the telephone's moonlit world. It's silent.

'Leo?' Even more silent. 'Leo, are you still there?' A deep grief-stricken sigh. 'Don't be angry, please. I have to do something for Father.'

'Ah.'

'Oh Leo . . . What have you written since I last saw you?'

'Nothing.'

'Of course you have. Can I read it?'

'No, I never write anything. Just odds and ends,' he says, referring to his life's work.

'Oh Leo.'

'I hate you, Arabella.'

'Yes.'

'You wouldn't know, of course, you couldn't possibly know that the highest intellectual moments are also the highest in sexual intensity. So that it's somebody's mind that is sexually attractive to you.'

'No . . .'

'Good*bye*, Arabella.'

'Don't ring off.' All the fun seems to be going out of life.

'Why not?'

'Because . . . all the fun will go out of life.'

Presently the telephone says:

'It's no use. Thinking about you is just a waste of time.'

'It *isn't*!'

There's some laughter. And then some more. The telephone sings in a low, mocking voice:

'Ara-bell-a!'

'I'm here,' but as I say it I look hastily over my shoulder to see the butler going back with no lids on the hot vegetable dishes.

'No, you're not,' says the telephone shortly. 'You're a horrid, nasty woman. You're little Miss Muffet. You're *Daddy's* girl.' Finally after a few more spiteful noises, it says slowly and triumphantly: 'I know what you are. You're a *classical French pear*.'

Suddenly my father (of all people) appears glaring in the passage! I hold the receiver a little away from me in a guilty hand, unable to think of a word to say, and after a second it clicks off and there's the dialling tone as loud as a tiger purring between us.

Father's silent, and that makes me tremble even more violently. I put the receiver back clumsily so that it rings every bell it has, and blunder into the screens around Michael's piano on my way back to the dining-room, exactly as though I'd just got out of someone's bed. Father stops to adjust the screens, and with his death-mask face on follows me into a room filled with noisy, spoilt people, all talking at once with pastry in their mouths.

Lady Escott is half-way across the table with her meaty little white nose pointed at Buffy. She's dripping confidence into his bloodstream, all about her marriages, while he, the unmarried, totally ignores her and just eats, drinks and grunts. Whenever she talks I've noticed there's something sexual buried in the conversation.

'. . . and he gave me two perfectly useless children, well, one's not entirely useless, she lives in Florence and I can go and stay with her . . .'

Overhearing these words, Mrs Bennett and Mrs Derriman go on eating as delicately and attractively as before, but each stiffens somewhere deep inside herself in her attitude to her children and her husband. New possibilities appear in their lives. Derriman and Eric Bennett would quite like to get into conversation with Lady Escott, or into bed with her, and each makes a mental note to say casually in the car going home: 'Who was that *awful* woman you were making friends with? Lives in Eaton Terrace? (What? Number 84?) Typical. Empty-headed, a real troublemaker. I should steer clear of her if I were you.'

I try to make up for that phone call by talking, at the very last minute, to Eric Bennett about horses. To my amazement he doesn't seem to know much about them. I encourage him by inventing amusing, semi-ignorant comments on the subject:

'I find it difficult to stay on. It's like a bicycle, there's nothing to hold you up. And when they bend over and eat grass there's just a hole in front of you where the mantelpiece used to be.'

Buffy suddenly turns his head and snaps at me:

'You're trying.'

Eric Bennett looks gloomier and gloomier. It occurs to me that he must have lost a good deal of money on his horses, and I'm rubbing salt in the wound by reminding him of it. He's a one-sided man who only really thinks when he thinks about money; the rest of the time he plays, like Michael or myself. He says with strength:

'Show-jumping is the most terrible racket. The horses are injected, cocaine in all four legs in advance, they can't feel a thing and they're terrified. I'm getting out of it as quickly as possible.'

Father has heard, and makes approval signals. There's no end to Eric's decency tonight. All at once Buffy is back with us again, red sideburns riding on his jaws; he says briskly: –

'I'd like to have these allegations investigated if you could supply me with some names.'

At the idea of supplying someone with some *names*, Eric Bennett drops his serious manner like a red-hot poker which has only just that minute burnt him. He laughs affably.

'So would I, believe me. If I knew them, I'd do the investigating myself.' He smiles around at us.

'But at least you must have some idea where to begin? All I would do, would be to leak the story to *The People*, and they'd follow it up from there.'

'Buffy,' says Eric with absolute sincerity, 'if I could you

know perfectly well that I would. I loathe it as much as you do. Who doesn't? Good heavens.' He leans back in his chair and makes a direct challenge. 'What sort of a man do you think I am?'

Evidently Buffy must have frightened him to death with that reference to *The People*. All businessmen know that any publicity to do with their money is bad publicity. I often wonder why Eric hasn't got himself knighted, and I suddenly realise it's because he's too rich. In any case, with his honest eyes he soon has Buffy backing down and hacking away at his food again, an occupation he should never have left in the first place.

'Well, I don't think you're the Mafia,' Buffy says, querulously, still putting Eric on the spot.

'Neither do I think you are,' says Eric, roaring with laughter at the thought. He's obviously in a blind fury at being taken to task at a dinner party. Father is looking so hard at me that I know it's my duty as a woman to change the conversation; he can't risk interfering himself or they'll turn on him and bring to light that the butler, the cook, and old Mr Chorny have cocaine in all six legs and he, Father, makes them jump through the hoop on Sundays instead of going to the cinema. There's always something you can leak to *The People*.

'Talking about the Mafia and Sicily, Buffy, did you ever finish reading *The Leopard*?'

'Finish it? Of course I finished it. I always finish books.' That, of course, is his whole trouble; he always finishes books. I know that if I wait, an opinion will follow. He says in a beautifully stuffy voice: 'I consider it to be the greatest novel of the twentieth century.'

'Oh! *Buffy*. A work by a prince to do with heredity, titles, and possessions.' Teasing Buffy is the only good reason for a long, dull, English spring.

'I suppose you think it inconsistent with my principles . . .'

'Certainly.'

'Well, I've examined my own attitudes, and I don't find it so at all. He couldn't help being born a prince. I would have picked this book out if it had been written by a Durham miner's son.'

He's getting further and further into the mud, and although I've performed a necessary service for Father, I mustn't let Buffy go under, which he's fully determined to do. The only way to stop it is to be serious. I make a tremendous effort to remember what Michael said about the book, and go after it, haltingly:

'I remember Michael said the book only began to be itself when you were about a third into it . . . and that its real originality lay in a fresh layer of sensibility, which was intellectual not sensual, in which worldliness was integrated with high ideals in passing judgments on life . . . and this was . . . a genuine artistic achievement, because it was done without drama . . .'

Father says pleasantly from the other end of the table:

'That's enough of that.'

He won't back me up, but cuts me off in the middle of a sentence. After years and years of backing him up in conversation and laughing at his jokes and finding what he says interesting, this conversational ingratitude sticks in my throat. He doesn't even say 'thank-you' with his eyes for the fact that I've drawn off Buffy and left his precious

Eric Bennett intact. I really believe he thinks he's done it all himself. Father has too large an opinion of himself, which is unfortunately fully supported by everyone else.

Half-way through the raspberry sorbet, with some really good fresh raspberries, it occurs to me that I rather like Buffy now that he's let me tease him in public, and I look for something to say to him. But I make the fatal mistake of returning to the same subject:

'By the way, do you agree with Michael, Buffy?'

He can hear me perfectly well, because Mrs Derriman has just leant back to let the words go by her. He says nothing for a second, and then takes an exceptionally large helping of cream.

'It's been a cold, snowy winter,' says Buffy with a snow-filled profile, 'and the weather hasn't really broken yet.' Which means that he liked me, that I've injured his pride, and that he'll never, never forgive me. At the same time it also means he doesn't have to stick to home ground at the dinner-table any longer, having trounced Mrs Derriman and myself, and he at once strikes out for the Domodossola of Father's end.

I'm now thoroughly disheartened, finish the meal in near-silence, and take the women upstairs to a little morning-room, in which everything imitates a proper bedroom. My own is too much like a fragrant dustpan to be used. I'm always curious to see how women will behave at this moment in the evening. Some of them fall to pieces, slam down handbags, shout, and knock each other over, while shouting 'Sorry!'

Mrs Derriman and Mrs Bennett relax slightly, and one can see what a relief it is for them to be away from their demanding, note-taking husbands, but they remain in control and relatively gracious, still bothering to finger their beads. Not, I now realise, at all secure. Whereas Lady Escott is all over the place, caftan, shoes (yes, muddy), handbag. She's soon found out that it's not my bedroom, and horrifies me by running down the corridor girlishly to find mine, and *finding* it. She seizes my lipstick and quickly makes a to and fro red shape on her mouth with it. Next the scent bottle. She twists the little glass stopper, frowning peevishly to get it out, and then slaps the liquid up the insides of her arms as boldly as if it was surgical spirit. 'Oh, I love scent, don't you?' she asks me, gaily. I'm so surprised I just stand there watching her go through my things, making a mental note to throw away the lipstick tomorrow. How could she come upstairs straight from the raspberry sorbet and vulgarise my lipstick like this, just as if we hadn't fed her? I can't use it myself now. I'm squeamish about having my personal objects touched, and Lady Escott seems to be all lips and fingers tonight. I suppose that's what absolute financial and emotional security do for you. She's taken hold of my plastic bottle of sleeping tablets and looks in through the wall to see what they are: Soneryl. She shakes them at me like a rattle: 'Bad for you! And what's this?' It's a little electric night-light made in Italy. I feel as though I'm being laid bare; my inability to sleep in the dark, all my fears, are at the mercy of this Buffy-lover. What does she do next but pull open the drawer of underwear because it isn't closed tightly, and she can see something with lace on inside. 'How pretty! So fresh and virginal.' My skin crawls, and I'm only just in time to stop her reading my Wolfs telegram. 'Oh, a love-affair! Who is he? Must be in a hurt, sending you telegrams. But you even keep the envelope; how sweet.' For a woman with a good complexion, there are moments when she can look incredibly blowsy. And this is one of them. I know that I'm in danger, and that this woman is going to take something away from me, unless I'm very, very careful. My father?

Later that night Father says: 'In future we must serve hot *or* cold soup.'

7

Wolf, Wolf, I want to see you after the letters and telegrams, and you're late.

Tea begins at three-thirty here, and it's already five past four and all the other tables are full. Raised on this little stage at the Ritz, people are pouring out tea musically into little cups while the fountain runs. There's a good deal of pink and yellow about in the corridors that lead away on either side, but up over our heads it's airy and light as an aviary waiting to be painted in tempera by Tiepolo.

Ten past four. Still light and airy above me, but I've taken in the atmosphere, removed my gloves, have my chin resting on my hand, and need a companion, compliments, chivying, or just straight, interested, sensual nagging from my Wolf.

No Wolf.

I go to my diary, to make sure it's the right day. Of course it is. And the right time. More than the right time, it's beginning to be the wrong time. I'm surprised that a man who sends greetings telegrams should be late. Slightly ruffled, I take out the letter I'm writing to Michael, and look about for the transparent rod of a biro. Ah, here's my old friend from yesterday, I recognise it instantly because

I've managed to make an isthmus of the black clip that points down from the cap by pinching it very gently near the tip between my front teeth. I take hold on the thoughts in the letter; there's a long list of books Michael wants from Dillon's. This translation of *Lucien Leuwen* by Stendhal (but for Baudelaire's work it would have been the most intelligent book of the nineteenth century), how am I to get hold of it? There's a gritty morning in Cecil Court in store for me, and up and down the Charing Cross Road in dirty fresh air.

Suddenly my Wolf is twenty-five minutes late, and I order tea for one abruptly, and put down my biro.

He's going to stand me up. Unbelievable, but true. Again I'm surprised at myself to find that it's a gigantic shock. My heart drops out of my side, but – I go on living. I'm no longer part of a happy gathering of civilised people pouring out tea, I'm an animal suffering from shock, as lost as though I'd been left behind stranded on a mountainside. There's desperation in all my gestures, and I'm unable to think at all about anything, any more than a wretched lamb is, running in that especial higgledy-piggledy fashion, as they do when lost, and bleating. I seem to have lost contact with the outer world; it's a form of madness. I make some mechanical gestures over the teapot, touching things.

Why on earth has this been done to me? Was it premeditated? I think back to month-old behaviour. What did I do or say that earned me this? It's only when the unexpected enters the expected order of events that you go back and try to find fault with yourself . . . and then you're at his mercy. God knows we both behaved badly enough; we certainly tried. And bad behaviour is so erotic.

I no longer look over my shoulder eagerly for a six-foot man with thick hair. I do not expect him. I eat some cucumber sandwiches, and although the brown bread is delicate, they clot together in my throat and I can only just get them down. There are some threads of watercress on the plate; I eat these for no reason and then realise that an enormous painful tear has gathered in each eye because I can't really see the flimsy stalks of the watercress from the other side of the hot, swimming water. I mop it up quickly, horrified, and make up a cup of dark brown tea and drink it firmly so that it souses my emotional throat. I'm so hurt that I have to make a rigid plan of action for myself, which I must follow to the letter in order to get myself out of the hotel. Now, call for the bill, pay it at once, another swallow of scalding ugly tea, and then pick up your things and go. (Was it because I wouldn't go to bed? Or because I said no to dinner and stuck to tea, bearing in mind that I shouldn't really go any further with a married man?) The stupid thing is that I still feel affection for this man, I haven't yet reorganised the internal machinery; I know this affection grows out of my love for Father, which burns underground and makes it possible for me to feel for another man. I have, in advance, the habit of loving this kind of man.

For one minute I think I'm going to have a migraine. These always start by a loss of focus, and then the familiar zigzags of light begin their dance from the side of one eye, until gradually they cover it almost completely. Fear, depression, and panic bring this on, and they make Father so angry that I've learnt to control them and to get rid of them in exactly twenty minutes.

Even if my Wolf turned up now I probably wouldn't even see him, always provided I was able to see against the migraine. I'm fixed on salvaging my dignity and getting out. I touch the long jade necklace that matches the jade-green jacket I'm wearing over this black maxi-skirt. Of course, green. I might have known this would happen. Certain clothes are always unlucky for me. The jacket has three small buttons running down from the neck, and as I make sure these are done up by going over them with one finger, I'm aware that someone has come up to the table and is standing looking down at me. I've *just* begun to think my own thoughts again, beginning with that absurd reflection about green, and this gives me enough presence of mind to look up at the arrival.

It's my Wolf, large, much larger than life, dark coat, gloves, half-smiling face.

I can't really take in the fact that he's there. I peer at him uncertainly. The hole in time and space I've just crawled out of was too real, much more real than he is. I look at my watch to try to fit in this figure among the new events – I mean my departure, the paying of the bill etc.

'I know. Thirty-five minutes late.'

He sits down. I behold him while remaining motionless and without expression. I don't feel at all angry; I'm just beginning to feel a faint relief at the edges of the numb areas, but I know I've got to be angry or he'll do it again, if I ever give him the chance. I say with vitriol on every word:

'*How could you be so monstrously late?*'

He bows his head and goes on smiling, and says:

'I know, I know. Don't tell me.'

I'm coming back to life, and to my great relief I find I'm trembling with rage, now that there's a real person to be enraged with. Thank God for some feelings I don't have to invent! The suffering I've just gone through is out of all proportion to the importance of this man in my life, or to the situation.

'Could I have some tea?' He's asking for tea, sitting there with his overcoat and gloves still on. My rage has strengthened me and I'm cold and calm. No one could guess that I've just shed the bitterest tears into that watercress.

'Got stuck in the tube,' he says in a slight, off-hand voice.

I've decided that this is the last time I shall see him, because the crazy emotional see-saw he induces is a bad augury for even the most temporary relationship. When men begin to behave badly, they gain more attention than you would have given them in the ordinary way, and for this reason you become fixed on them. I want to unfix myself, and I give myself *carte blanche* to be as rude as I like to him. I've still got my AC, Michael, Father, and my duties. I return mentally to these things, and murmur:

'Amazing.'

A quick waiter brings up an extra cup. How like a waiter to wait on you when you don't want him.

'Could I have some?' My Wolf touches the cup. He doesn't look directly at me; but then he never did.

I pour cold brown tea into the cup. Then I replace the teapot, and immediately feel about for my gloves saying as I do so:

'And I hope it slops all over you.'

I know directly I've said it that it's too young, too schoolgirlish, and that he's going to laugh. And he does.

That's the last straw; and I stand up.

'Are we going?' he asks, standing also.

'I am.'

I start to move away, going slowly in order to keep myself in one piece both physically and mentally. I don't look back, but I know there's some turning about and wallet-fumbling. In no time he's beside me, and is following directly through the glass doors. I get through these doors carefully in my long skirt, because the Ritz seems to breed young men who knock you over. They're always running up the steps, late for some assignation; once inside they disappear completely and you'll only find old men roaming the corridors. My Wolf is a case in point; after all, he's only been loose indoors for five minutes, or less.

I've come to love this English arcade outside, it's so ugly, almost as bad as an arcade in Zurich. But still it protects you from the roaring of the rest of London.

We walk a few paces together, and I say, almost to myself:

'I must get my car.'

'Where did you leave it?' he asks, picking up my tone exactly.

I decide to do something feminine, and wave my hand nowhere.

'Over there.'

'I see. Well, we must get across the traffic.'

Now there are some men who are so good at getting women across traffic that it's a form of love-making, in which the woman is touched, protected, and lifted forward, until she reaches the opposite pavement in a state of mild delirium. My Wolf is one of these. My hand, my arm, and my shoulders receive any number of deliberate caresses, and these have their effect. I am, after all, close to a male body I have been thinking about comprehensively for well over a month, and being unable to protect myself with conversation, I'm receptive to the size and darkness of the figure and to the alert, hostile head that never looks at me. Oh yes, crossing Piccadilly with my Wolf is much more dangerous than a whole evening in a nightclub with him. On the other side he snaps out:

'Now where?'

'Berkeley Square.' I've got enough stamina left over from the Ritz *débâcle* to add bitingly: 'Under a tree.'

But I'm losing ground, and I know it. For as we go forward it's my Wolf who sets the pace of our walking and I who hurry to keep up with him. In no time he'll have me saying 'Sorry' for something; no doubt it'll turn out in the end that I was late for him.

There's always a drawing-room light in Berkeley Square; one is never out of doors, as in the open country of Regent Street with its savage winds. In the yellow electric light here some people are sitting about on seats. Here's my red dog of a car, parked in a gigantic ash-tray. Under the windscreen-wiper is the familiar yellow docket in a polythene bag. I rip it off the glass but slowly and with style, and then stare at it instead of hiding it away. The language and literature of this yellow fine, glass-housed against the rain in a coat the colour of rain itself, is bestial, rigorous. The typefaces used on it are those of plain bureaucratic juvenilia.

Since this is exactly what my Wolf expected to find on a

car parked by myself, he stands in an I-told-you-so attitude. I've no intention of explaining that I forgot to put any money in the meter.

'Got the keys?' he asks.

I unlock the car silently and prepare to get in, ostensibly leaving him standing on the pavement.

He looks at me. I look at him. A car is a bedroom, or if not that, it's at least a sitting-room.

'Are you going to give me a lift?' he asks casually, throwing the sentence up towards the workman's hut which is the daytime entrance to Annabel's.

'Which way are you going?' I say it to make difficulties so that whatever his answer I can reply that I'm going in the opposite direction.

'Your way.' This is uttered with a necessary sharpness.

I open the passenger door, and he gets in and sits there. No movement.

I'm not quite certain what to do, so I start the engine, and immediately the car takes over. As soon as I back her out, it occurs to me that there are no seat-belts for him, and that the only place where I can make my Wolf shudder is up on the M1 and even there with the speed restrictions I shall have to drive quite badly. I decide to do this, and turn north, giving her a burst so that she backfires. And then just to unnerve him and to give me a reason to burn any oil off the plugs by speeding afterwards, I pull out the choke while we wait at a traffic light, so that she's overchoked and makes a ghastly sodden, wallowing noise. It hurts me to do it but I want to hurt my Wolf more. I catch sight of myself in the driving mirror and notice that I have my Viennese governess face on again: I want something, and what I want is sitting beside me. Like any puritan I'd rather die than admit it, but the mouth in the mirror is almost bitchy, and inwardly I'm full of hope. I've got rid of that thirty-five minutes of pure suffering in the Ritz by the time we reach Swiss Cottage, and my Wolf has twice looked for something to hold on to. I'm driving impetuously but too well, and have begun to forget my passenger in attending to my mechanised alter ego. I've just remembered, though, about the bald tyres, which make the project slightly dangerous.

'You going up the M1?' asks my Wolf, in exactly his Berkeley Square tones.

'Thought of it,' I answer pleasantly.

'Could you pull over for a minute?'

'Oh. Why?'

'Tell you in a minute.'

We have to slow down because of traffic, and my Wolf takes the opportunity to say:

'I'm afraid I've got to stop. In that lay-by, please.'

I pull over into the lay-by, but keep the engine running. My Wolf at once gets out.

'You getting out? No?' He closes the door and walks around to my side and opens my door. 'Come on, Arabella.'

Uttering my name like that surprises me; evidently he's someone who knows me quite well. I feel human for a moment. He bends down and switches off the engine which is so damaging my behaviour. Without the noise and heat of my anaesthetic, I'm grounded and perfectly happy to get out. Directly I'm out he slams the car door and takes my hand and walks me off, swinging my arm briskly backwards and forwards as you do a child's. Where? We're in no man's land. Just grass with concrete edges. We walk on the grass, I can hear the long stems slapping against my polished boots. There's a corrugated iron shed and actually some kind of field with a gate into it.

'Oh good. St James's Park,' says my Wolf.

For a moment I think he's going to look for some kind of latch by which to open the gate, but I underestimate him again. No such nonsense. He rests me against the gate and puts his arms around me. I'm overcome by shyness, and he responds by kissing my eyelids. Oh God, he's kissing me with affection; I hadn't allowed for that. Again the soft, fragrant face close to mine. The effect is to lull me, and make me sleepy exactly as before. The more slowly something is done the more powerful and erotic is the effect. There are opium dens in North Africa where a big carpet, impregnated with some narcotic, is very slowly shaken over the heads of those who seek oblivion.

Then my Wolf kisses me on the mouth, and I'm back with the lover in the motor car of a month ago. First the harmless dry boy's lips which seem not to know their task, but know it better than any. And again, on my side, the same feeling of exhaustion and near-despair that I shall never get to the centre of this kiss. It's so bad this time that I do in fact murmur: 'I can't stand it.' And he murmurs back: 'Oh yes you can.' This second kiss is much kinder, gentler than the first. It's not an all-out bid, but a method of communication and reaffirmation of what our meeting is about. His mouth tastes nervous. When it's over I rest against him, very tired after my labours. But as I rest, I'm astounded to hear again that refrain in my ear:

'When will you sleep with me?'

It's as though nothing has been understood; no thought has been given either to me or even to himself. For if we were actually to go off now, straight away, and get ourselves a hotel room, and make love, the results would be disastrous. Lives and love-making depend on timing; there's a moment which is absolutely right, and that moment shakes the world. How can a man who kisses like this not know these elementary facts? Possibly he doesn't know what else to say, and since this is the one thing on his mind, he says it, over and over again.

I'm suddenly reminded with force of those thirty-five minutes at the Ritz, and my reply has the breath of suffering and sarcasm which I brought away from it.

'Don't bother to get to know me,' I say to the coat-sleeve which encircles my head.

The body of my adversary receives the words, arrows which go in in total silence, and we remain in one another's arms as though nothing had happened, like an old married couple. I'm only waiting for him to break away and look at his watch, now that he knows for a certainty that there is nothing to be obtained from me in a quick shopping expedition where you buy things over the counter.

He does break away, and looks sternly at me. Then he bends over me, and quickly and without warning he kisses me shortly, deeply, and fiercely, inside my mouth. And then outside it, holding my mouth entirely enclosed by his with such tenderness that I'm blinded by love and lust, and a form of temporary security that makes me timid. This kiss is so satisfying that there's not a word to be said afterwards, and we both walk back to the car together, concentrating and perfectly separate, as after a good meal.

All right, Wolf. It's established; you can kiss. Yes, you took my breath away with that last kiss; I admit it. There are some kisses which are in themselves sexually satisfying, and there are others which are so incomplete, they aggravate the nervous system, fray the temper, induce such great longings that they can never be satisfied, and so on the whole do harm.

I drive back to town, and the silence is unbroken all the way. We're both digesting the information we've received. At Marble Arch I remember with a start that I promised to make carbonnade of beef for Father tonight, and it takes two and a half hours. Too late; it's already nearly seven o'clock. Father must have arrived home. I get into Hyde Park and stop the car. I can feel the old nervous agitation coming on. I say to my Wolf:

'I'm so sorry, I've got to go.'

'Aren't you going to have dinner with me?'

'I'd love to. But I can't tonight because I promised my father I'd be back, and there's no one else to do the cooking.'

'Well, let him cook for himself for once.'

It's hopeless to go on with such a conversation. My *raison d'être* in Father's house is as housekeeper. I can keep any appointment, go anywhere, so long as I give notice of it, but I can't leave him disconsolate to forage about in the refrigerator and to walk through the large rooms on his own with a coloured drink in a glass and no one to nag. No; it's unthinkable. And if I do go out there are always notes, almost letters, left for him, a good three-course meal, and a cheerful cook in the kitchen who's instructed exactly how to wait on him.

'I really can't tonight.'

We're suddenly very close, closer than we've ever been, talking away to one another about something real. I realise that my Wolf has taken my hand and buried it away in his coat, against his chest.

'Why wouldn't you have dinner with me?' he asks, seriously.

'Because . . . I thought I ought not to.'

'Then why have dinner with me in the first place?'

'I wasn't sure whether you were happily or unhappily married.'

'I'm happily married.'

'Oh.'

My own unhappiness hits me with redoubled force. Every day I carry my life forward steadily, hoping for an improvement, waiting and watching, and what my Wolf is doing at this moment is increasing my insecurity. At the same time he gives the impression of being permanently angry because I won't go to bed with him; or else this way he has of being slightly rude all the time is the means he employs to show people he's intelligent. My own sophistication is of the emotional kind; even when frosty and dressed up, I will go out of my way to avoid hurting people's feelings. But there are fits of bad behaviour when I'm irritable, afraid, or late, which perhaps do more harm. And I'm late now!

What's this gaze from the passenger seat? Sincerity, authentic emotion, from a happily married man? And one who's endangering my precarious foothold at home by every minute he keeps me there. Oh, if I'm going to have a man I don't want someone else's; I don't want borrowed shoulders, borrowed hair. I give myself a little shake from irritation, and ask:

'Well, what's a happily married man doing here?'

'I'm not monogamous.'

'Rotten.'

For this I get my head gently kissed again. It's this gentleness which is unnerving. He's too close, the narcotic we make between us is too luxurious and gripping. He says, muffled and hungry:

'Why did you let me kiss you?'

'I – thought about you in advance.'

'Tell me.' (The 'tell me' has a note of despair, as though he's drowning.)

'I thought about your mouth.'

'What?'

'What d'you mean "what"?'

'Why, then.'

'Because it was . . .' I start to laugh because the real reason is that it pouts a little, the mouth of this angry Wolf, but I don't see how I can tell him so. I look at him drowning there in the passenger seat because no one's ever told him his mouth pouts (and does it beautifully). Instead I see Father's face, and I call out sharply:

'I must *go.*'

What on earth has happened to us that we sit here talking confidentially, as though we are friends?

He says decisively:

'I'm going to pursue you, Arabella.'

'Nonsense.' I start the engine. 'It won't do you any

good.' I'm anxiously wondering what to do with the beef, which is really only fit for a casserole. These realities make me say something real, and it is:

'I'm not going to see you again, Charles.'

He gets out of the car, looking away as before, and says in a quick gabble of honesty, which disturbs me:

'I go with extreme reluctance.'

I drive away like a whirlwind, pulling out stops on the dashboard to get the maximum speed and noise out of the organ. I imagine my face is grim, and my mouth a mess, as though I've burnt it eating over-rich food. If only the small change of domestic life in our house was a little bit less exacting, if the service did not have to be quite so perfect, I'm sure I would be more balanced in my judgment of the men I meet. But I cannot see clearly because of the harassment, and I keep making escapes, instead of initiatives towards a life of my own.

The faster I drive away from him, the more deeply and surely do I know that the die has been cast in this relationship. It was cast the moment the palm of my hand met the palm of his. It's the instant your fate tells you you are going to do, or not do, a certain thing . . . at breakfast, say, between putting down the marmalade and picking up a cup of coffee. But I don't like the relationship, it's wrong, it doesn't feel right, I disapprove of it and of myself. Wasn't that evening supposed to be one harmless, frivolous evening away from problems? I shall do everything I can to obstruct the relationship. I certainly shan't see him. And I shall begin at once to look for someone else. In no time, being the proper Wolf he is, he'll pass on. And at least my conscience will be clear, for the more you get to know a man the more you get to know his wife, and I'm beginning to think that after all she must be . . . rather nice . . . when he stops snapping at me.

You'd think that Father could find me some men in his profession who weren't married. Or does he do it deliberately – leave me alone with the married ones?

'There you are at last. Where on earth have you been?'

'Shopping.' (Anyone would think I was his wife.)

'What, at twenty-past seven?'

He's sitting bolt upright on a pale blue chaise-longue at the end of the sitting-room with his arm in a black sling.

'Oh Father, what have you done to your arm?'

'Neuritis. I've had it all day. It's absolute agony.'

I kneel down beside him on the carpet, long skirt hampering me, and put my head against his arm. He looks at me like a resentful child whose mother was missing at a moment of crisis. I say with my burnt mouth:

'You poor thing. It's too bad. I'm going to make you a solution of Epsom salts and hot water to bathe it.'

He stirs impatiently.

'It won't do any good! If we had meals on time and a bit of organisation in the house, I wouldn't get these nervous tension pains. Really, Pigeon, I can't stand it. I'm under the most frightful pressure making decisions all day long at the office, and then I have to come home and do the housekeeping. It's too much. I shall have a heart attack. You'll drive me to it.'

'Oh no, no, no. I'm so sorry. I'll get dinner at once. Sit there gently, Father. I shan't be a minute.' At the door, I say with reproach in my voice: 'I'm not usually out, you know.'

'You're out more often than you realise.'

Directly I've left the room and run down the passage to the kitchen, I can hear him saying something else in that way he has of finishing his sentences even when there's no one in the room. I stop and call out anxiously:

'What is it?'

The sentence seems to be being repeated in exactly the same conversational tone of voice. I have to go back to listen, and re-enter the sitting-room.

'I'm sorry I couldn't hear you.'

'Oh not again!' He's really irritated. 'I was simply telling you that you'd rucked up the carpet when you came flinging your way into the sitting-room.'

So I have. That little tapestry carpet under the chaise-longue. I must have caught it with my foot when I knelt down. But really he's sitting right on top of it, you'd think he could do it himself. I suppose not with one arm in a sling. I run to pull it straight and as I do so he looks at his watch and fixes his lips in displeasure.

It's a painful evening, and we don't speak. I cook and serve the meal as unobtrusively as I can. It's bad and has no taste. Father asks for pickle, mustard, Worcester sauce. At the end of it, he gets up abruptly and says:

'Now will you please get a couple to live in.'

I've noticed that the two places where Father gets angriest are near tables of food or dance-floors.

He goes up to the bathroom and brings down a tin of indigestion powder, which he mixes up in a Waterford hock glass in the kitchen. While he's sipping it glumly, brooding on the misery of his existence, I try to find a remedy for his arm.

'There's an analgesic balm upstairs we could try. Won't you let me rub it on for you? It burns at first, but it numbs the pain. You know if you go on having pain, Father, you get into the *habit* of it, and then you sort of manufacture it even when it's not there.'

'I'm not manufacturing this.' He's very short tonight, but allows himself to be led upstairs to the medicine cupboard again.

I'm delighted to be in charge, and start giving instructions.

'Off with your coat, and please roll up your sleeve.'

Father sits on the bathroom stool, big, with his handsome bald head watching me, and fighting off a heart attack due to arriving home first and not finding dinner ready.

I fuss over him. His arm, now that I see it close to, is a fantastic object, as solid as the round branch of a beech tree. It's covered with black hair, growing in an elegant pattern. He allows the balm to be rubbed into it, looking at me peacefully like a lion taking a sunbath. I replace his shirtsleeve and do up the cuff-link, which means more fiddling over his wrist. Finally he gets into his coat gingerly, and rearranges the black nun's sling. He enjoys it all, and even tells me what time the pain came on, and shows me the only position – if he holds his arm up like that – in which he doesn't get it.

The fact is that I've got my father into the ways of women, and he couldn't now do without an interesting feminine subculture in the house, with absurd bath caps, bedroom slippers with fur on them, little French china pots of cosmetics, and a sewing basket with hundreds of pockets containing *diamanté* buttons from some fancy dress of the past. He says that when I talk to him about his vests I make them seem important.

And yet for me it means 'Arabella, don't do that' or 'Come *here*, Arabella,' from my father or my Wolf alternately. I can even imagine my Wolf ordering me about in bed, if we were ever to get there: 'Turn over. Get into the right position. Behave yourself, but not too well.' Between the two of them, they give me such a low opinion of myself that I can't imagine anyone finding me attractive.

When Father overwhelms me with domestic tasks I've often wondered whether it's because he wants me to leave home and is driving me out, or whether he wants at all costs to keep me there by giving me so much to do that I can't roam abroad. And yet he's very keen for me to be financially dependent on him. Whenever I suggest taking a job, he says: 'What on earth for?'

He doesn't at all like it when one of my very few friends comes to visit me. But curiously enough, instead of leaving me alone with them he'll come and sit with us in a silence broken by curious, off-putting remarks. Until they finally get up and go, when he at once tries to detain them in conversation. I've come to the conclusion it's because he has to prove to himself that they come to the house to see *him*. And, in these circumstances, he does his best to entertain them – although of course he doesn't really want to, because they don't interest him. The idea of someone coming to the house for any other reason is quite unpalatable.

Just as we're going to bed tonight, Father stands in my bedroom doorway. He says flatly:

'Pigeon, are you or are you not going to get rid of that piano?'

As usual, he's taken me by surprise. I'm in the act of folding up my clothes. I haven't prepared my ground mentally for defending Michael, and you have to be absolutely sure of your ground with Father.

'Oh – well – I haven't –'

'You promised me you would, and you haven't done a thing about it, have you?'

'Did I promise?' I'm puzzled and unsure.

'You asked me to leave it to you. And I leave it to you, and this is what happens. Nothing.'

Now if I answer: 'I'll see to it tomorrow,' Father will assume I'm going to get rid of it. It's infinitely safer to say nothing. There are times when I know him better than I know my own soul. Suddenly I can hear Father's voice in my head, murmuring with pride to Eric Bennett: 'He's gone for some religious experience.' It's almost as though he can read my thoughts from the doorway, because he ends the conversation quickly with the parting shot:

'It's me or the piano.'

8

Michael writes that the move out of the Portland Hotel in Karachi into the desert will be the best thing he's done so far. He says the servants in the hotel shout all day long, and the other residents scream at them from wooden balconies. Apparently there's a railway station directly beside it, and heavy steam trains, years old and overloaded, chug very slowly away up north to Lahore. He says the heat and noise of these trains is unbelievable, and it sounds as though they're being driven through the hotel. There are no doors in the hotel, just jute mats, so that any breath of air from the sea isn't lost. He says he sits under a fan, wet all over from the heat and itching. He keeps cutting his feet due to wearing badly fitting sandals, and says he has carelessly worn a pair which have forced the nail into the flesh of his toe, the left one, and now it continues to grow in. He says the city is dry as dust and smells of camel. At nights there is a brown sky, due to the dust that lies over the city, and a creamy moon. He says that as he writes to me an ant has just run past his writing things on the way to a piece of chocolate he left out without thinking, and that there is a water shortage. The water is turned on once or twice a day and the lavatory cisterns go mad. He says it's agony not to be able to wash. He says that staying alive in Pakistan is all a matter of posture: you must be languid. And he isn't.

His letters don't contain news in the ordinary sense. His idea of news is imaginative and philosophical progress in his head. It's only by nagging at him, just as Father nags at me, that I manage to find out these physical details. But after the enormous deeds he does in his mind, he says he finds the things of ordinary life very easy.

I'm in the same mould – except that I'm embedded in ordinary life. For example, while I'm stacking the washing-up in Father's large Colston, I take a number of important decisions about my life and feel as though I've covered hundreds of miles at one jump. But when I've finished and closed the machine by its chromium handle, all I've actually done is to stack a Colston! Less absurdly, I do have a way of waking up in the morning with the light pouring into my head on some piece of truth about someone that I never understood fully before.

I'm writing to Michael as usual. It's my daily task now. I give him psychological *earth*, so that he can get his roots into it, and never feels lost. I make him a present of an hour of my life every day. Really these letters are miniature novels, in which I re-live certain events in his company. I'm almost incapable of writing a short letter – to anyone. When it's finished, my letter to Michael, it needs an air-mail envelope, and there are days when I have to 'make' stamps for it. This means getting old fourpenny and tuppeny stamps off corners torn from envelopes which were never sent, or printed business-reply envelopes of Father's with free stamps stuck on them. Then you assemble all the odds and ends together, find you're a penny short and the post goes in five minutes – so you run like hell, maxi-coat flying, to a distant post-box with a stamp machine on it with a little brass lip. There's always an east wind blowing when you catch the post, and often sleet showers which swoop down and pour heavy drops on your fragile document. You always meet people you know who assume, from the speed you're running, that you want to get into conversation with them. I once met Buffy, who actually *ran beside me* to prove he was my age, and kept glancing in an addled way at my bosom because my coat was streaming out and tossing behind me. (Still it was better than meeting him in Bond Street, because when he walks there's a great deal too much lurching from side to side, and if you stand still to talk to him, he promptly falls over.) For all these people it's a game, but I am carrying life to Michael in these letters, news about clothes in the King's Road and Biba's, who I saw at the Aretusa, what Leo dredged up from Soho conversations with spiteful old imitation literary men, who's in the psychiatric ward, who caught a flea at the Paris spring collections, the fact that there was a real horse in Act IV of *Boris Godunov*, who was lunching at Wilton's and avoiding who, any piece of gossip or a newspaper cutting which might amuse him.

In return he tells me that he can't sleep because his greatest desire is to get out of himself a modern lyric which will run with his blood, and in which his blood will supply everything, intelligence, even organic rhymes under the full pressure of emotion. He'll do anything, *anything*, to get such a poem. He knows it can be done, and says Shelley nearly did it. He says he's assembled the pieces, and now he's going to make the diabolical strength to fall upon them – and will I please tell him something bad about Father so that he can reconstitute the old rages which were so good for his work and put all his values in sharp blacks and whites. He says that the really amusing thing is that when he's accomplished what he knows to be the most difficult task in the world, *not a soul* will know what he has done. He says that even the preliminary thinking other poets do is wrong; the laziness begins there, with clichés of vision. So far as he can sum up his old life in London, he says everyone seemed to turn on him on account of the poetry, they simply became enraged by it – in the way that people are chemically enraged by their parents, wives, brothers etc. – and that the stupidity was so terrible that at moments he thought he was going mad. 'Are they wrong, or am I wrong?' was the question you asked yourself in England, says Michael. But he goes on that those who have never left the safe streets of England, never succeeded on any other level, will never know themselves. In Karachi it's better because you're up against real life as brutally as you are up against real poetry, and the two are indivisible, both being literal. So that at least he's in one solid piece again, and not being broken into and demoralised by Philistine versifiers who are a hundred times more destructive than Father. (Michael and Father are rapidly becoming indispensable to one another.)

He says that although on the map he's not really closer to Russia, he feels closer, and that there is more Russianness in his daily life. And that's what he wants. Russia is the great love of his life – there is a depth of soul which is absent from contemporary England. You've only got to mention Osip Mandelstamm and Michael's body goes completely rigid, in case the wrong words are said about him.

This Sunday morning I put down my biro and the white block of paper, and suddenly run downstairs into the street. It's one of those beautiful white European mornings – mornings that I noticed for the first time in Paris, when I saw the edges of the paving-stones washed mauve by a river shower which had just that moment come over from the shady trees of the Ile St Louis. Yes, I'm walking on these Holland Park pavements and seeing everything with Michael's eyes. It's so fresh, it's just the morning for getting arrested and being marched away and never having to think again. I remember with deep love a poem by Michael about the cinema which begins: '*I frog-print the nuclear jam into your vulnerable girl's hand./All the real life I've had, I've stolen this way.*'

Good Lord, I actually forgot all about my bed-ridden, happily married Wolf. I really don't want someone who blows a hole in my life for no very good reason. It only makes my bed emptier.

I return in a hurry to the house. I know that Father disapproves of this strange lingering on the pavements, and I've had my ration of whiteness for the day. As I enter the short drive, I hear someone playing the piano close at hand. One of the neighbours perhaps. But there's a gap of at least thirty feet between the houses . . . badly, but lightly and quickly go the notes . . . it's coming from our house. Don't tell me that Michael is – Oh, it's Father.

He rises from the stool instantly, caught. (Sling hanging empty!) I have pity on him and ask, as though it was the most natural thing in the world:

'Is it in tune?'

'More or less. It's better than I thought it was going to

be.' He starts to replace the screens. And then to show me that his reason for touching it was purely commercial, he says: 'You might get twenty pounds for it.'

He puts his arm around my shoulders and we stroll a few steps together in the hall – I catch sight of us in the big mirror, Father and daughter, two emotional, stubborn faces smiling at one another with love and guile. These little scenes we play out together for one another's benefit, they're essential when two grown-up people live together. I know that all Father's moods are due to his anxiety to get even with time and money, and to satisfy a few urgent needs on the way. He must have moments when he thinks, as I do about my Wolf: 'Shall I take this bit of life, because if I don't I may not have any life at all?' No; his existence is not as precarious as mine.

'We need a music-room,' Father is saying thoughtfully; 'you could convert my old study on the first floor. It would make a very pretty little music-room. And then we could have some musical evenings . . .'

Musical evenings! Father is always building on some new wing to his imagination which I had never foreseen. This is what comes of a *tête-à-tête* with Eric Bennett; two bold, wealthy Philistines pretend to one another that they're pining for musical evenings. We'll be running up a chapel in the garden if Father and Eric get any closer.

'By the way, Pigeon, did I tell you I've got these TV people coming here in three weeks?'

'Not exactly.'

'They won't disturb you. They'll only be here for a day. I'm supposed to dictate letters at home, according to them!'

'So they're filming *you*?'

'And the furniture.'

I like the way he says they won't disturb me. Of course it's only his way of putting it, as though I'm bound up in some iron household routine of linen-counting and bread-baking and get ratty if I'm dragged away from it for one moment by frivolous, good-for-nothing cameramen. Possibly he's suggesting a role to me? Florence Nightingale of the linen cupboard. I'll play it with pleasure if it keeps him quiet and makes him happy.

I suddenly realise why he wants a music-room. He wants it for the same reason that he wants Eric Bennett to know *why* Michael went to Pakistan. He wants a public soul. But why? It's quite unnecessary, when he's such a good man. Has he reached the age when he has to prove to himself he's a good man? Father, what on earth have you been up to in the past?

Of course he can have his music-room, in three weeks, just in time for the TV cameras. I'm so touched by his vanity that I kiss him warmly, and he kisses me with extreme sweetness on my head in return (just like my Wolf). We say not one word about Michael's piano, which gave him the idea in the first place. But it's true to say he lives in a certain way, because Michael changes him just by being alive. He must know that my terms for making a music-room are that the piano should remain. Perhaps a superabundance of pianos is what he wants at the moment. We say nothing and go off in different directions.

No, I don't want a Wolf hole in my life, but I find I've started thinking about him without realising it, behind my other thoughts. Each time I do this I have to make the same mental decision to give him up, and it's beginning to tire me out. *He's* manoeuvring from a position of sexual and emotional strength. Whereas I could not be more vulnerable, and my only security is my thought. I find myself going through my meals alone as though I'm making love to my plate, my wine-glass – this I lift up to my eyes, give it a long sexy emotional stare, and then drink it down fastidiously. Not content with that my fingers go up and down the stem in a desperate and gentle manner. I touch my napkin and the edge of the table as though they were the cloth of his clothes and the hard form under the clothes. This is accompanied by a piercing sex headache. Luckily the headaches are so beastly that you throw away all these thoughts in a bad temper . . . but not until they've brought you to your knees, taken away your authority, broken you, and used you up in ten minutes. It's something to do with the honest quality of the conversation in the motor car, it's unnerved me, and the sexless affectionate head kisses. Until that moment he was an enemy in dark coat to be driven up the M1 until his teeth rattled as the bald tyres went over the cat's-eyes. And that insane refrain: 'Will you come and sleep with me?' like a disembodied computer's voice which only has one sentence for coping with such a standard situation. Until then he was *anybody*, kiss or no kiss. But now he's a real person, and it's the real people from whom you suffer in life, because when they're taken away you're much more lost than you were before. And it's the real people you think about.

During the weekend I can't finish a sentence, entirely due to these thoughts which will think themselves the moment I'm off duty.

On Monday at breakfast the cleaner has put the letters by my plate, and there's one from my Wolf. I open it, smiling a little in anticipation, and read the good white paper. I read what amounts to a dismissal. I've always been slow in picking out the actual core of the message from a letter, and whether it's friendly or cruel. And this one, which I expected to be a suggestion for a theatre or dinner somewhere, after a formal greeting says to me: 'Shall we call the series a draw, do you think?' and goes on: 'Let's see each other now and again – not too soon, though' and is signed with a single initial 'C'.

So *that* was the level on which we were operating. How shallow, how despicable. I feel green and fall in my own estimation, that I should not have seen through a man who was merely having a series – a series of matches with an emotional score-card. Evidently I wasn't scoring heavily enough, wasn't looking pretty enough to get my own way – if that was my own way, to eat grass all alone in the Ritz for tea and to be kissed in a horrid concrete lay-by off the M1. And I had just been disembowelled by what I took to be honesty but which was all part of some well-acted, cold, amoral game. And this man I thought to be *un*sophisticated is evidently so sophisticated that he won't be bothered with me a minute longer, since it's now perfectly clear that I can't be got to bed. He won't stay the course. But how malicious to make sure I desired him and to build himself as deeply as he could into my system before cutting me off.

What's this about 'seeing each other now and again'? As though I'm to have the pleasure of a sight of the horrid pig walking through some drawing-room in the distance, just to keep me going on the days when there's no gravy in my life.

I look at this letter, which shows me how other people think, and I'm astounded that it can be written by a grown-up man complete with leather gloves, wife, and large position in the City of London. It's so spiteful that I have difficulty in attaching it to the last piece of behaviour of my Wolf, so close to me in the car, saying hotly: 'I go with extreme reluctance.' Of course you must never, never pay attention to words said, but only to deeds done. And this letter is dictating goodbye.

I instantly re-plan the sort of thoughts I want to think in the future, like a convalescent who must think himself well. After a poor breakfast, I go upstairs and find the old greetings telegram in its drawer of underwear, and remember that I slept with it in the bodice of my nightdress because I thought it meant love and goodwill. Nothing of the sort. It meant sex or the end. And I might just have well have slept with a page from Krafft-Ebing.

I heartily regret every caress, every kiss, regret the burn in my coat, regret wasting my jade necklace, all thrown away on the wrong person and spoiled.

So that's how things are outside in the world. Father has always warned me that I wasn't sufficiently hardened and have no idea of what really goes on: people being rude to one another, ordering one another about, writing letters about calling the series a draw etc., etc. I shiver and return to my anxieties, for who knows, if my Wolf ditches me like this, that my father won't do the same?

The only good thing about the letter is that I have this unknown wife off my conscience, and that's important. I hate other women suffering, just as men hate other men to suffer.

Do I write back? I suppose so. I write back and say 'all right'. Otherwise he'll think I'm hanging on for a last few emotional scraps, like a little dog, forlorn, whimpering under a table. And he'll have to keep his word and 'show' himself now and again. I must prevent that at all costs. Goodbye then, Wolf. You've taught me not to trust so easily, at least.

Part of my convalescence means phoning up Leo and Buffy to see whether I'm still alive. They're both grumpy and smarting. Buffy goes straight back to *The Leopard* and argues his case. It's incredible from a clever man. He's a snob with a working-class chip on his shoulder, and he genuinely doesn't know it. What a bore; I hold the phone away from my ear while it snaps and crackles with snobbery. When I go back to it, it's telling me an anecdote about staying in a cheap hotel in Palermo, and to rub in the cheapness of the hotel Buffy is *again* sharing a bedroom with his father:

'. . . my father lay down on the *only* bed, it groaned and at once all the cupboard doors flew open and a bat circled round and round overhead.'

I suppose this is why one ends up with a Wolf.

Leo is even worse. He's in the middle of one of his gigantic depressions, and can't go uphill to the fishmonger's to buy his kippers because he's afraid the hill is going to fall on him. The difficulty with Leo's unhappiness is that he gets a positive appetite for tragedy, and it begins to take the place of joy. From me he has to have his ration of tears, hysteria, neurosis, before he feels he's even 'got through' to me. He asks very tenderly after Father, and says he needs a very great deal of love, implying that I'm not giving it to him. Then he says he's completely exhausted and rings off.

Neither of them will flirt with me, both seem hostile and try hard to snub me. There's nothing for it but to plan Father's music-room.

I go about it with a dull mind today. There's no weather outside, just empty spaces between the houses. I choose, up on the first floor, one of the spare bedrooms, in preference to Father's study, and go in and stare at it. Blue silk curtains with a heavy nine-inch drape along the floor would make a music-room of it in no time. Lots of little gilt chairs for listeners to listen on, a Victorian button-back chaise with bolster – maybe in scarlet silk for colour TV? – for Father to lie upon with his arm in a black sling, signing stock transference certificates with his free hand and glancing at a score on the music-stand beside him in between, just like Mozart. We must have pencil drawings on the walls, so faint you can't see quite what they are, a photograph reproduction of Beethoven's crossed out dedication to Napoleon, and a tiny pornographic drawing in sanguine on the other side of the piano, framed in black onyx. An enormous china jug with rough country flowers in it, chrysanthemums and leaves. Oh and the largest mirror I can find, and if possible a real fire burning – to give the impression we're in an upper room in Imperial Vienna, feeding ourselves on music and blue silk to keep out 1970 London.

I'm quite inspired and walk about the room, humming. Music already!

I make a long shopping list of these exotic odds and ends, and drive slowly down to Sanderson's showroom in

Berners Street. (Wolf, Wolf, I miss you, and realise it was my own unpredictable behaviour that contributed to the split between us.) I feed my parking meter mournfully, and as the sixpences go in and the clockwork machinery fizzes, I realise that I'm again giving to Father two more hours, three more weeks, after the ten years I've already given him. I wish I were giving them to myself, or knew how to. It might make Father a great deal happier if I did. I see how it is; I'm still trying to create the role of daughter, when that role is finished and I'm a woman.

Inside the showroom I catch the eyes of various men and women, torpid and haggard as drug-addicts, as they turn over the endless fabrics. I have never actually seen a face with an expression on it in this showroom; blanks, and more blanks with dead eyes. The suffering is awful, and it goes on and on, like writing out 'I must not say *bloody*' a hundred times at school, until you're free to rejoin the mainstream of life. Perhaps Leo's depressions are like this; he wanders about his own mind picking up and putting down various thoughts, each one newer than the last, incapable of making a decision about them. I suddenly make a decision and escape.

Outside I'm aware of the shops. *The shops!* Hot boxes of glass containing new clothes, new life, with which to find yourself a new man. Quickly! I've just wasted ten years and two long kisses, so naturally I'm in a hurry. The King's Road. My car loves a purpose, and we go down Park Lane on the scent of it.

There's the most beautiful park in the world on the right, with its vistas of blue fog and cambered flower-beds, filled with false plants with thickish leaves, white edges, and a heavy fur pile. But it's Rotten Row which matters, due to the way the green leaves flicker about and the slow motion of a shiny horse cantering nowhere. So different from the motion of the women, raised up on those hideous shoes which are in fashion at the moment. Every time I look in the window of a shoe-shop I start humming: 'Clump, clump, clump, the boys are mar-ching.'

Through the Hyde Park terminus of new blue roads, avoiding the underpass with a straight mauve shadow lying across its entrance like the unpolished blade of a guillotine. Cars accelerate at the sight of it, and go down there full tilt into the electric cavities to be brain-washed by the twilight and to emerge brand-new, weaker, while the tunnel goes on roaring at them ineffectually from behind.

I give the last drop of my energy to parking in Chelsea. You have to be as old and clever as the city itself to park successfully along the prohibited, treacherous coastline.

I wasn't going to see my Wolf again anyway; and what I am doing is 'the right thing'. In any case, such a man will never love deeply enough to make the kind of love I want to make. He'll always be marking a score-card; abysmal.

Yes, but why is every pavement filled with facsimiles of him in dark coat with that springy black hair on top? I had no idea there were so many of them about. Evidently it's a London type.

Straight into the first boutique for my cure. It's dark in there and so noisy I'm afraid I may pass out. I acclimatise and start drifting between the racks of parrot-coloured clothes like Shadrach in the burning fiery furnace. Every tiny piece of clothing has a couple of huge labels on it, suitable for a cabin-trunk going to Australia. When you try things on these labels scratch you to pieces.

In no time what was a burning fiery furnace a second ago now turns out to be my natural element. It's more like dark water, and I glide about as if I'm going around a coral reef in an aqua-lung outfit, detached, looking at things, getting scratched, all the time thoughtlessly floating and drifting on.

My attention is suddenly riveted by the sight of a strange woman with her hand on something I want. Horrible! I'm ram-rod stiff, just like Michael in a poetic fit. She's turning it over (a very pretty midi-coat in white felt) and pinching it in her fingers, acquisitive cat. If she goes on much longer, I shan't want it myself. Why can't people leave things alone, when they're so obviously unsuitable for them? I try to draw her off by showing enthusiasm for a nearby rack full of belts and chains. Directly she leaves the coat for the belts and chains, I acquire it and disappear into a velvet decompression chamber which smells of urine, to try it on. Under these appalling conditions, I manage to buy one or two things – and the amazing truth is that the clothes are smart, fit me, and suit me perfectly, as though I myself conceived them and as though they had always been mine. I always love the latest fashions and exactly the same thing happens every time.

I emerge, young and happy. Goodbye again, Wolf. You see, I'm as shallow as you are, sophisticated, stupid, sensuous and cold. At breakfast I lose a man who interested me, but by teatime a new set of clothes has quite put him out of my head.

9

'They'll arrive at eight-thirty. The cleaner can let them in and tell them where to go. No need for you to be bothered.'

'How many of them, Father?'

'Oh I don't know. Half a dozen, perhaps. I shall come back from the office directly after lunch.'

'Will you prepare anything to say?'

'Not especially, but I have been asked to speak my mind, and I shall take the opportunity . . . whether women should be allowed on the floor of the Stock Exchange,' he says it to banter me, 'and other topics which might amuse the public.'

'Why shouldn't they? Is the floor uneven?'

'It is a bit!'

Equal again: Father should have been more careful when he gave me his kind of mind. Or are we simply dovetailed into one another?

By the time I go down to breakfast the following morning, there are electric cables running across the hall and upstairs. I follow them into the sitting-room where five youths in jeans are stretched out on the sofa and in the chairs reading magazines in silence. No one looks up, and

I have a sensation that I've entered the wrong room and in someone else's life, and almost go out, apologising. In the hall lavatory, a strange girl with blonde hair is making up her face with the door open.

When I've finished breakfast and leave the dining-room, she's still there doing exactly the same thing. I daren't speak to her because she's so busy. I put my head into the sitting-room and the scene is as before. The only sound is the crackle of magazine pages being turned over by the young men who are concentrating.

Since I have accounts for the Chelsea conversion to be done, week-end orders to be given, a cleaner to be paid and praised, I leave the camera crew and go upstairs.

I can't resist looking in on my music-room; a triumph of phoniness, accomplished by bribing a local upholsterer, by getting deep moulding laid on the back of the door, by transporting materials myself by hand, by attending auctions to obtain the boudoir grand, and by hiring men to carry Michael's piano upstairs. There it is, at the back of the room, ugly and old, but still the true heart of the enterprise. Those gilt music-stands are so elegant; the pile of music isn't really high enough, and it all looks rather new, except for some sheets of Michael's with his writing all over the margins. The television crew have fastened some rose-pink jellied paper over the windows, and switched on a very powerful lamp which gives a glowing pure white light, a lump of light, making one think of one's childhood ideas about arch-angels. A little fire of red coals keeps absolutely still in the grate. I walk to and fro in the room on my own, enjoying it, as though I were in an indoor garden with some heavenly presence. Suddenly it occurs to me, as I walk here alone in the limelight, that I am proud. And immediately after that thought, I stop in my tracks . . . *Michael.*

What on earth am I doing here, enjoying a room, playing at musical peacock, when Michael is desperate and unhappy in Karachi? I know that he is, although he doesn't say so. And recently – after a description of his desert flat – there has been a long gap in his letters. In fact, I haven't had one for . . . all the time I've been at work on this room. The day I bought these gilded bamboo chairs was the day of the last letter.

I go at once to my room, and taking it out of my little walnut davenport, I read it through anxiously. Yes, he walks, still having foot trouble, every evening as the sun goes down to the sewage farm which is behind a hilltop building which people call the Aga Khan's summer palace. This sewage farm is emerald-green in the middle of the brown desert; it's only when you're close to it, says Michael, that you see that the channels which feed the orange trees carry the blackest, strangest-looking water. When he takes a turn around the house just before going to bed, there's either brilliant hot moonlight or a whole sky full of twinkling white stars going right up over your head in a navy-blue vault. There are wild dogs which howl all the time at night; vultures, crows and falcons. Every window in his flat is open to catch a wind. If it comes from the sea it will be humid and he'll pass the days with sweat running off his elbows as he writes and trickling down his chest. If it comes from inland, he'll dry up and crackle like a parched lizard and there will be grit and sand between his teeth. At night he lies and tosses under the fan, soaking wet. The catches which hold the windows open are already rusty and they make a curious fretful, squeaking noise as the wind blows. He has a lazy bearer called Abdul.

I long to rescue him, not only from the desert, but from his own mind, which took him there in the first place. But his inner world is so strong and interesting that he prefers it to ordinary life. It even seems to change the quality of his flesh, as sophistication does. His imagination never sleeps for one second, and I know it's this which makes him physically and mentally ill. He has entered a condition in which *everything interests him* – is there anything more alarming?

I re-fold the letter with great care, as I've been doing for the past couple of weeks (the joins are so grimy), and put it away again. I look out of the window and tap on the top of the desk with a biro, wanting to write to him with fresh suggestions, stories, warnings about his foot, but I'm not able to. The gap in letters is too long. And there were no letters again this morning . . . or were there? Did the cameramen pick them up? Of course! That is exactly what must have happened.

I hurry downstairs and look about in the hall. Nothing. Back into the sitting-room, where nothing has changed, just as though it was being filmed. I wonder whether I dare to interrupt these technicians. Standing about looking at them isn't having any effect. So I begin quietly:

'Could I ask something?'

A boy with brown ringlet hair and his shirt undone to the waist looks up wearily from his carnal magazine; his lids are still half over his eyes.

'Yes, dear?'

He is bored, calm and rude. And I notice that he has exactly the same lack of expression that I saw recently on the faces in Sanderson's showrooms.

'It was simply that – we don't seem to have had any letters this morning. I wondered whether anyone had picked them up ?'

He goes on staring at me, and then he slowly shakes his head from side to side, and drops straight back into his magazines as into a trough. No one else has even raised their eyes, and I'm just turning away, when one of them, the one in a canary roll-top sweater, clouts the magazine he's reading with his fist and throws it down, completely disgusted.

'Apollo!' he says. It's a copy of *Apollo* magazine. Evidently something in it wasn't up to standard.

'Letters . . . letters you say?' He has nothing else to do at the moment, so he stretches out his hand to the backgammon table, on which rejected material – the *Radio Times*, the *Economist*, *New Society* – is lying unread. They seem to have been sorted over for readability, and he quickly does the same again, in case there was something in colour on shiny paper that he missed. Ah, a small sheaf of letters, only five, but better than nothing. He hands them to me with a kindly smile, like Zeus not wanting to be bothered with correspondence on a morning when his creative instincts are running strongly.

I take them without a word and leave the room. I fly upstairs away from the horror of the sitting-room which has been transformed into a third-class railway carriage where youths with candle-grease faces sit endlessly reading magazines, eating Smarties, and throwing down orange peel. I even lock my bedroom door to keep out the image.

Then I go over the letters, trembling. Two typewritten for Father, one . . . for me, in my Wolf's hand. Oh! I don't feel strong enough to open it. More insults, surely. There must have been something in my reply that annoyed him again; even as I detach myself from this man, he's going to criticise the way it's done. And now, what are these curious buff envelopes, suitable for sending out bills in, with Pakistani stamps on them, badly addressed by typewriter? Both to me, but date-stamped three days apart. I take the latest, and rip it open.

'. . . I write again to you, Michael's sister, because he is not able to write at this moment. But he is making very good progress. I come to see him every day, and he asks me to tell you not to worry because the worst is over, and now there can be nothing but recovery. He does not want his father told, and he keeps repeating this. Although personally my opinion is that he shall come home as soon as he is well enough to travel.'

Michael, Michael, what has happened to you? Oh I can't breathe, there's something wrong with my chest.

I open the first buff envelope and it tells me that Michael has poliomyelitis and has lost the use of the upper part of his body and of his left leg. There is a signed chit from a doctor, stating that there is no reason at all to suppose he will not recover partial or full use of the affected areas.

I am lying half-across the bed as though I have been stabbed and pinned to the bedcover by the weapon. Michael, my little baby, who trusted me, and who was so beautiful and so proud of his body. Oh Michael! You're still there, still alive then? but broken.

I leap off the bed and start pacing up and down like a

crazy woman. I must get him back *at once*. I shall fly out there. For this I need money, something I don't possess. My old responsibilities settle on my shoulders; I must scheme for Michael again. The prospect of a life for myself disappears forever, and I take up the old burden willingly.

I must have *details* at once. For if he can't move the top half of his body, how can he feed himself, or dress, or wipe the sweat off his face? And who will do this for him? A lazy bearer called Abdul?

In imagination, I recreate from the last grimy, much-folded letter a picture of Michael lying on a bed under a fan, motionless, near a rusty, squeaking window and surrounded by books . . . *which he can't even pick up*.

And how can he pay the doctor? Is he getting the medicines he needs? Is he in pain? *How much* pain?

Now the first thing to be done is to obtain money for the flight there and the price of two returns. My only source of money is Father, but Michael forbids me to tell him. Obviously because he doesn't want to give Father the satisfaction of coming to his rescue, and saying: 'I told you so.' And then Zoë could go around for the rest of her life jabbering about 'kitchen-sink' poetry. I start pulling open the drawers where I keep my few pieces of jewellery and my fur muffs, and in my distracted state I pull out anything that I think I can sell. Then I remember the car; two hundred and fifty pounds at the most, with the gears sliding around as though they're in a pot of treacle and you have to hold her in third or she spits the gear back at you. My good old friend, my red dog who lives for herself, who will want you with the broken music you make? Only an idiot like myself, who can't bear to drive slowly.

What else? My grandmother's gold locket with the ruby in it, some little rings, my Cabochon ruby ring, and that cultured pearl one which is too small to wear nowadays. Anything else ? My clothes, one or two Courrèges things, Dior ball-dress, lovely but not new.

It's not enough. I shall have to ask Father. Suppose I fabricate a white lie, say I need five hundred pounds for the Chelsea house? Suppose I just ask him for it, housekeeper's wages for ten years? Oh Father! When I think of the way you *clung* to me when you were weak and insecure after Mummy's death; every day I had to tell you you were handsome and clever until you believed it, and when you were ill I'd get up in the night to listen outside your door, to try to hear – by the way you were breathing – whether or not you were asleep. And if you tossed about, I'd go in and give you a sleeping tablet and resettle your head on the pillow. And now you tell me, on a mountaintop in Switzerland, that I'm pathetic and have a line on my face. And I can't ask you for five hundred pounds.

Yes, a fit of self-pity and sentiment. Still, it's over as quickly as it came. I see how to go about it: I'll collect a little money here and there, without fuss. It'll take a few days, that's all.

Even in the middle of my anguish, composing these minor plans is a refreshment. I feel better, and able to leave my room. Why, when I came in through that door only ten minutes ago Michael wasn't paralysed. Now he is; I live with the news, and grow around it as the oyster makes pearl. But the whole texture of my life is changed radically, my thoughts are bound together as they were that evening on the Moubra when the ice cracked. I can no longer remember what it was like ten minutes ago to live without a purpose.

I unlock the door and in the corridor I run into another TV man. I suddenly find I have a loathing for tousled men. And this time I'm perfectly ready with dead eyes and a dead face of my own. He's put off for a minute, as the two unbaked slabs of pastry meet, but there's something like a glycerine fish-twinkle in those colourless eyes, so that evidently I've begun to learn their curious language based on apathy and staring one another out, which Michael and I used to do as children. Not only have I learnt it, but he wants to break into conversation.

'D'you mind if I use your piano . . . in the music-room? I work with a group.'

It never occurs to him for one instant that I could say no.

He thinks I'm going to fall on his neck and worship him because he 'works with a group'.

For a moment I can't speak because I'm overcome with emotion at the thought of Michael's piano, which of course he can no longer play. So I nod to indicate that I do mind, very much, if he uses the piano. But nobody's ever said no to him before, with that double passport to nowhere which he holds, his image as a TV producer and his image as a pop musician, and which allows him to turn everybody's house into a railway carriage. And so he nods and goes on in the direction of the music-room.

I manage to get out a curious lump of words:

'I'm afraid the felts have gone, and the piano shouldn't be used.'

That holds him with one foot in the doorway, and he hangs there for an instant, and then turns about and slouches off downstairs, glowing with hostility.

Father returns directly after lunch, as he said he would. The house at once comes to life. Father courts the candle-grease youths, he is so unassuming and affable that they ask him to come in and sit down. He gives them the impression that he's lucky to know them and is already benefiting from it. He seems to be humbling himself unnecessarily, and I have an uneasy feeling he'll do anything they ask. If they ask him to beg for fish like a seal, I really can't see him saying no.

I know I'm looking terrible, and keep catching sight of my distraught face in different mirrors. Father passes me on his way to be made up and says:

'What on earth is it? You look as though you've seen a ghost.'

I can't explain. Perhaps he thinks I'm nervous on his account. I feel I ought to reassure him; after all he has to 'go on' in a few minutes. I go to the door of his room and stand there for an instant.

Father is sitting very still on the upright chair by the tallboy, while the blonde girl from the downstairs lavatory goes over his face with a huge powder-puff. He looks idiotically happy, submissive and fulfilled; if purring was natural to human beings, he would be doing that, but instead the sound of a very similar clockwork breathing, which I normally associate in him with deep sleep, fills the room. The girl, who smiles as she works, is silent. Dab-dab, dab-dab, and then lipstick, which it seems Father's lips have been waiting for all these years. I suddenly realise, as I spy on them like a ragged phantom from another world, how masculine make-up is.

He's seen me, and waves contentedly, without speaking. When it's over he rises slowly to his feet, smiles broadly at the girl, dusts down his waistcoat, and passes between us, patting me as he does so and saying at the same time:

'Your turn will come in life.'

He thinks I'm envious!

The rest of the day is a nightmare. Every time you go near the sitting-room, dining-room, any room, Father is standing in the centre of it talking to a camera. And yet the camera crew seem to be filming themselves all the time, or rather they film their own ideas. They're in love with themselves, like five monkeys passing on fleas. I get out of the house with the odds and ends I think I can sell, and stow them in the car. I haven't the slightest idea where I can find a pawnbroker, but I decide to try Bond Street silver and jade merchants with the better things, and then drive down to the East End. It's obviously better to go in the morning, and then I can call at a travel agent's to find out about tickets.

I write Michael a long, long letter. And I'm just about to carry round to the post office a parcel of books which has been waiting done-up in the hall for two days, when I wonder who is going to open it and who is going to turn the pages of the books.

All these thoughts and chores I do with a dizzy head, so much so that I break off in the middle to think about Michael and forget what it is that I am doing. I'm stricken, as stricken as Michael is, and can think of nothing else.

Much later in the evening when the cameramen have at

last gone, when Father has dined, and I've cleared away and am wandering about dejectedly, trying to take a grip on ordinary things again, I remember there was a letter from my Wolf.

And with a cynical little movement of my mouth I climb the stairs once more to find the letter, which will perhaps take my mind off my great grief for a second, with an insult or some other corrective.

There it is, on the pillow, under the silk scarves. I look at it. I'm in no hurry to be hurt again. I fold up the old scarves, one by one. Then I take up the letter. Same Wolf writing, upright with generous loops on the g's and l's. How misleading it is.

Just a moment, I'm not strong enough, not grief-stricken enough after all. I can remember him. I'll light a cigarette; I've seen other people do this in films at moments of agitation, and there must be something in it. I've never been good at holding cigarettes, I know I do it unprofessionally, and that's just how I'm holding the Nazionale now. I open the letter with a sad noise which my throat seems to utter of itself at the thought of lost love.

There's a sheet of dense writing, which seems to be a sort of diary of his recent activities. I quickly turn over. Yes, there, about the middle of the second page, is the information: 'I have been busy forgetting you, but what with all this forgetting you have been every day in my mind.'

For an instant, I relax with a feeling of hope, but quickly stiffen like a dog which senses it is going to be attacked from a new angle. Is this a free gift of affection – for *me*? No, surely, it's just sexual regret for the one that got away – that is, after being dismissed.

I read it again. He refers to his three-week-old letter. 'Please forget it.' I'm bewildered: how young his manner of expression is, as though we were both twenty, saying to one another: 'Sorry, didn't mean it.' It's his method of disarming me, of course.

But I see everything through a veil now, at second hand. It's too late; I'm already committed to Michael. There's nothing left for a London Wolf. In a few days I shall be gone. He closed the door on the relationship, and it was always a bedroom door. Now he seems to be trying to open a sitting-room door, so that we can have a friendship perhaps and discuss paintings? Yes, certainly, after kissing one another like despairing lovers, all we really want to do is to discuss Bonnard.

From far away at the bottom of the house I can hear a noise, that of a heavy door being shut and again shut. In a moment I know what it is. It's the door of the big refrigerator in the kitchen. And that must be Father investigating it to see whether it's been defrosted recently. He always does this when he's over-tired; there's an odd compulsion to find a white growth of frost, or if possible an old bag in which purple-green potatoes have started white sprouts.

I run downstairs, knowing that it's far too late to have a bad conversation with Father. He won't sleep.

Just as I thought. With an expression of squeamish disgust on his made-up face, he is carrying the large pan of the chiller to and fro, emptying chunks of ice from it.

'Really, Pigeon, it's too bad of you, letting it get into this condition.'

I stand there hopelessly. I know I have to be in attendance.

'And there's something that smells very bad indeed. You put your head inside. It's poisoning all our food. I don't know how you can open the fridge every day and not notice it.'

I put my head into the white interior obediently. I know he won't be satisfied until he's 'rubbed my nose in it'. There are some pork chops at the back, under a glass cover. I lift them out, and removing the cover, I sniff them expertly in a way that any cook-gourmet will understand. Father is horrified: it's indelicate to sniff meat like that – just like, well, like a dog. It's too primitive for him, and his senses are outraged by such a full-blooded mannerism in his own daughter. He thinks I must have inherited it from my mother, and he murmurs: 'What a little primitive you are,' to show me that he had no part in such alien behaviour patterns.

Oh God, why do I have to stand here and be forced to jump through a hoop at twenty to twelve at night when Michael is so ill in Pakistan?

I suppose because Father has been jumping through hoops himself all day and wants to obtain some similar satisfaction on his own account before going to bed. I realise though that I haven't heard that irritable tone of voice for – oh, a long time, at least three weeks now. These three weeks which have passed so peacefully are taking on an ominous quality. The very moment I've outlived my usefulness in creating a music-room, I'm found fault with. All the bad side of my character is noticed, and the little good I have done is taken for granted, after all it's part of the house now, as if it had always been there. And what was so difficult about using a little taste? Hasn't every woman as much or more than I have myself? It kept me out of mischief; I have no friends of my own, and no profession (as if somehow these things were equated with 'mischief') on which to spend my youth.

For the very first time in my life, a question follows these commonplace and very familiar thoughts. Is my father trying to get rid of me?

I watch him rinse out the chiller tray. He seems to be taking away even my own duties in the house, my domestic authority, the only thing I have left. I feel empty, and I know that I must sleep to be strong for Michael tomorrow. I touch his arm.

'Father. Come to bed. You must be tired.'

My voice is so quiet that it quite frightens me. Someone else has spoken.

He stops playing and some of the frustration goes out of his profile, but he still shakes his head as if over a bad bargain and leaves the kitchen reluctantly, gazing around at so many tasks left undone or not yet thought of. He says:

'The whole house revolves around you, you know.'

'Oh Father.'

10

More letters. My whole life is being lived through letters at the moment. The following morning there is one dictated by Michael, and with a heart that nearly breaks I see at the end of it a curious crabbed piece of writing, in which every character has the quivering of a seismograph. It was done by Michael with his left hand, and looks from its wandering faintness of imprint as if it took him hours. He was right-handed before the illness, and had never been able to write a word with his left, so that the effort must have been even greater. But he does not say so.

What he does say is that he *does not want me*.

'I really don't want any emotion or fussing over. I just couldn't take it at the moment, things are too serious and I feel I'm hanging by a thread. Don't be upset. It's more peaceful with strangers.'

My eyes hurt. I am upset. But I do understand.

I sit at my breakfast with everything cold on the table, my coffee with a puckered skin half over it, my boiled egg opened at the top and left. I re-read and re-read this bad typescript, so kindly done by some Pakistani poet who has befriended him. The details are *awful*, even unbelievable.

At first he found some difficulty in walking, so he went to bed, feeling feverish. He found himself twitching involuntarily all night, and just lay where he had fallen, half across the bed on his face. In the morning, he found to his amazement that he could not rise. He managed to call out, and his bearer came in and turned him over. He got the man to prop him up on some pillows, and there he lay all morning while the bearer went on foot to Karachi to fetch a doctor. The doctor (a very good doctor, the typescript is careful to put) said that it was just a temporary paralysis, no doubt due to typhoid fever, and injected him in an attempt to immunise him against the typhoid. His bearer fed him with a teaspoon and carried him to the lavatory, where he had the greatest difficulty in urinating and had to remain there for anything up to twenty minutes on each occasion. This state of affairs went on for five days, with vomiting throughout, and on the fifth day his bearer brought him a mirror and showed him his face. The muscles on the left side had become paralysed, especially those around the left eye, and from what he could see with his right his left eye had fallen as much as a quarter of an inch, and he was unable to raise the eyelid. On observing the condition of his face with one eye up and one eye down, he thought seriously of suicide, since he realised he could never pass again in civilised society in that condition. The doctor, who had been calling every day, told him that the eye would very likely right itself, and could simply be attributed to shock. Michael therefore gave himself twenty-four hours' grace, and had the mirror brought a second time. On this occasion he saw, and gave thanks to God for it, that the eye had righted itself, and although he could not raise the lid he decided to take the risk of remaining alive. (*At twenty!*)

The letter continued that his temperature then went down and left him as he was, able to hold a biro in his left hand; although unable to raise his arm, he could form letters on a horizontal pad of paper if it was wedged in beside him.

The next requirement was money. He needed a nurse, he needed expensive injections of vitamin B and treatment at the Seventh Day Adventist hospital. Would I send him two hundred pounds at once, and the same sum at regular intervals? Meanwhile would I please send him Rousseau's *Confessions*, Dryden, Boileau, Burns, Cavafy, Horace, Jules Renard, Giono . . . ? A long list followed.

As I read it, I am *almost* smiling. Everything is factual, real. The books are as important as the medical details. The smiling and the trembling that go on as I read this letter are quite absurd. When I read, a minute ago, that he did not want me, the words burnt, bit, and tore their way into my head. What he wants from me are letters – 'your letters are my lifeline' – and money. These letters I write to him take a lot out of me, there's an emotional draining, because I am giving him my life, and inventing something to give him since there is so little life. And he is taking it, as his right, because he depends on me and makes me responsible for his happiness; but he doesn't want me to take anything away from him in return, his time, his presence, even his sufferings – he must have them all to himself.

He's so like Father, who wants everything. Father wants me, wants a mistress (Lady Escott?), wants housekeepers, butlers, wants perfect living conditions, wants to be on

TV, he wants, wants, *wants*. He'd like to have five or six people just living his one life. Is this because he's reached a dangerous age? No, Father has always been a dangerous age.

But still, Michael's quite right. There's always a danger that you'll enjoy someone else's illness, and make a way of life out of it. So I have my own life back again, and suddenly a present of free time. But free time in which to worry, because without seeing Michael my imagination is let loose and the pictures it creates from these letters are horrific. If I let myself think about his left eye, I should go out of my mind. I keep dragging my imagination away from it and the mental action is as brutal as dragging a dog away from its food, so that I'm horrified at myself in turn.

The typescript pages are tumbled around my plate with the stone-cold breakfast and its slices of boot-leather toast. All I've had to eat are my own emotions. And now I must put together two hundred pounds, by borrowing and selling this and that.

The crucial point is whether or not I should tell Father. The only reason for doing so is to obtain money more quickly than I can on my own. I find I'm possessive about my grief, and don't want to share it with Father – I might lose some of it. Or perhaps I've simply become secretive over the years, since with a man like Father you never discuss a subject and go right down to the root of it. You comment on something from the surface and that is the end of it. Father always hopes that something awkward will disappear if he merely stops thinking about it.

And, far more important, I'm *out of the habit of taking*

action. I think this is due to the fact that I don't have a proper stake in life, in the world, and I can't therefore take on my responsibilities properly and react as I should or when I should. I have no spare money in my purse for this.

That first letter warned me that Michael should come straight home. Is it therefore *my duty* to tell Father?

I drive straight to South Molton Street, manage to park in it (a miracle since there are more parking meter attendants in this street than in any other in London), and within half an hour I've sold outright two of my pieces of jewellery. It's simply astonishing. I had no idea that things changed hands so fast. I feel light-headed and immoral, as though I've entered the *demimonde* and ought perhaps to sell myself into the bargain. After all, Father obstinately refuses to allow me to take a job, I have no other source of income, and he and I are not in one another's confidence. My only liaison, which I did not seek, has meant suffering; it would seem much more logical to strike a bargain with a Wolf of this sort in which you are paid for suffering, and much more moral in that it would relieve your conscience of anxiety with regard to his wife. The only one who would suffer from such a transaction would be myself; left high and dry, emotionally, sexually, and financially (since the money would go to Michael).

The moment I've thought these thoughts I stop in the middle of Bond Street. A sensation of total despair floods over me and I bow my head. I feel so lost, so terribly lost, that it seems as though I shall never find myself. I look around me, dazed. It's a beautiful sunny day. Well-dressed people are smiling at one another or looking into shop windows. Why is it that I, alone, am surrounded by difficult and demanding men who make me pay for everything, pay for every kiss, pay for my home, pay for my brother's health? I, who have nothing to pay with.

A voice from nearby says:

'Arabella!'

Oh no! I'm startled among my secret thoughts, lost inside myself, and there's a man, a stranger, standing beside me. Who is it? Everyone looks like my Wolf nowadays. I've lost all my self-assurance, I'm vulnerable and frightened. I look at him helplessly, only wanting to hide. Yes, I remember meeting him four years ago at a party. An eligible young man with black hair.

'How are you?'

I can't think of a word to say. I have two cheques amounting to three hundred and fifty-five pounds in my pocket, and I must get to the bank at once and transfer the money to Karachi. I mustn't lose one minute. I only stopped because my despair stopped me. I do see that I gave the impression of idle, carefree shopping, and so I search for something to say to go with it, but all my smartness has left me. I stutter, and then get out a sentence which turns out to be rather rude, almost a snub. He's profoundly insulted, and we separate, almost bleeding.

I run away, back to the car and to my worries. Doesn't this always happen, when the outside world, when new life, pushes its way in to me? I always say to it: 'Not today.' The present is so jam-packed with duties, and my head so packed with thoughts, that when I'm not expecting to see someone and suddenly see them, I can only half-see them and only half-talk to them as though they're not really there. No wonder I can't change the people in my life.

But Michael I can see inside my head all the time, every minute of the day, trying to form letters with his left hand on a horizontal pad of paper.

I queue at the bank, staring at the overcoat in front of me. I send the whole amount to Karachi, and outside again in the open air I feel easier for a moment. Then into the post office to send Michael a telegram to say the money's on its way. Another long queue of overcoats, old people so drunk with queuing that when they at last get up to the plastic mumbling grille (where you have to mumble everything twice anyway) they forget what they have come for. Some women unpack handbags and lay out objects as though on a bedside table. I can hardly wait while a poor dolt buys seven fourpenny stamps and holds me up for more minutes so that my life goes down the drain even faster.

Then it's done.

I enter a strange restaurant and try to eat one of those sharp meals they always seem to serve to you at moments of crisis, all pointed chips and a lamb chop with a great big L-shaped bone with L-shaped blubber on it. I can't swallow the food, if food it is.

Now for the books. The rest of the afternoon is spent at this toil, for I must serve Michael perfectly in everything. Until a year or two ago I loved bookshops; but as I grew up, I grew level mentally with some of the books inside them and the disappointment was very great. No philosopher, when read, seemed truly to philosophise; no erotica was really erotic; no poetry was ever poetry. After that, they were like cosmetics or vegetables, and I attended to other sides of life which gave me as much or more than the books. This was Michael's influence; he was no hammy book-worshipper, and the physical side of a book – the smell, the jacket, the meat of it – meant nothing to him. He cut a book open: if it lacked genius he threw it away or lent it to Leo; if it had genius he carried it with him and wrote all over it. The fact that he can't manage without books and never stops reading doesn't alter his contemptuous attitude towards them. 'I don't like the air round here, Pigeon, but I have to breathe it because there's nothing else.' That's Michael.

When I get back to the house I find the piano-tuner, another of the Mr Chorny sort, waiting on the doorstep. I take him up to the music-room and he settles down to a steady dong-dong-dong-dong, then up the scale then back, then dang-dang-dang-dang.

Father returns, wanting dinner early. The windows are open. It's June. Father remains slumped in the sitting-room for a long time, and has to be roused, as from sleep, before he'll go into the dining-room. Directly the meal's over he returns to the same slumped attitude, as though stodged hand and foot in blancmange. What is it?

(The dong-dong-dong-dong from upstairs is maddening.)

I go up to him, but he throws me off. Then I recognise the symptoms. Father is going to have one of his depressions. There's a lull in his activities, or he's been worsted in some deal, or he's just woken up to some new want; something has gone wrong and he's taken by his old fear of not making the grade in life. The symptoms are lethargy, sweating, obsession with detail in the house which runs concurrently with complete lack of interest in it and in his life, if such a thing is possible.

These depressions, which I associate with ambition, grind my nerves to a fine powder. A few years ago I wouldn't have put up with them for a second. But then I was much stronger, had many more friends, and had actually planned to leave on one occasion, I remember, when Father stood behind the big sofa, looking down, with the tears literally falling out of his eyes. We were both shaken to pieces, and the subject was never mentioned again.

What can I do with him? Time is standing still in this sitting-room. I look across at him, holding back my terrible secret, which grows heavier and heavier as I carry it about.

Perhaps I can distract him by talking over my sheer malice against the television men? But as soon as I've begun the subject I know it's wrong, because it reminds him of my strange behaviour in peering through doorways at him.

'But, Father, I was completely anonymous.'

'Like hell you were. You couldn't see yourself. Peering around the doors at me with a dead white face. You couldn't have chosen a worse moment for showing off. Really, it was just as though you wanted me to make a mess of it.'

'But it's not true! I only wanted to keep out of the way.'

He doesn't at all like the tinny way my voice has risen, and, turning his head to get away from it, he goes on lying there like a poisoned rabbit, saying:

'Don't *whine*, Pigeon.'

This is the beginning of some bad days. My everyday life has an additional layer of seriousness which it does not really need.

The typewritten letters arrive nearly every morning, like the pages of a novel. They wring my heart as I sit at my solitary breakfast, which I do not eat.

The part of Michael's body which is most affected is his right hand. He cannot move it *at all*. He cannot raise his arms or turn his head, and has to be propped up still since most of the muscles of his back are paralysed. *But* he can walk a bit once he's set on his feet, and if his bearer supports him, since the left leg has only lost power at the top of the thigh and the ankle, which means that he drags his foot and is unable to mount stairs. His right leg is unaffected.

The money has arrived! And I've already sent the next instalment. Michael now has a Eurasian nurse with strong brown arms, who comes every day. She washes him, feeds him by spoon (he says this is *hell*), gives him pain-killers and injections. He says that waking up in the morning – if people who are in constant pain can ever be said to 'wake' – is the worst bit of it. During the awful sleepless sleep under the fan in the heat, his limbs get fixed immovably into the position where they have been put, and they lock together. Directly he wakes he knows that he has to try to move them, and the pain is excruciating, because once he has started to move them he must go on and yet he cannot bring them back to life as one does a foot which has gone to sleep. He says the pain is very similar to a foot going to sleep, when the blood and electricity run back into the dead limb, except that it *does not come to an end*.

He dictates that his left eye is remaining in position, although the lid is still down and he is inventing ways of propping it open. A curious part of his eye trouble is that his eyes, like his limbs, get fixed in one position, and he has great difficulty in moving them out of this stare.

He says his doctor is afraid his limbs will shorten, because, apparently, if a limb isn't used it wastes and contracts. He can see this already because large hollows and holes are appearing all over his body. The doctor doesn't appear to know a great deal about the disease and says: 'Do what you feel you can do, but don't overdo it.' The doctor insisted on putting his right hand into a plaster-cast to keep the tendon stretched, but the position with the hand turned back was so unbearably painful, since the limb continuously weakened, especially the underside of the wrist which had no strength at all, that after three days he had Abdul cut into the plaster and remove it. He says it is already a battle of wills to remain alive against the doctor and against the nurse whose fixed idea is to get him into a bath.

Then he turns at once to the books. He has them piled up around him, with the good ones on top. He drags them towards him with his good hand, but if one of them falls to the ground, it's a tragedy and all he can do is to lie there and look at it.

For a day or two now he's been mentioning the possibility of an operation on his right hand. It appears that the body goes on attempting to send impulses into paralysed areas, and if an operation can be performed before the muscle wastes away, that flicker of energy can be directed and maintained, and finally converted into normal functioning – but only if there is still enough muscle left to react to it. So that once a muscle wastes away past a certain point, it is gone forever. Such an operation, entailing nerve-grafting, would mean returning to England at once. Michael says he looks at his right hand, which is now so tender that he cannot bear to have it touched, and wonders what he should do. He feels too weak to take a decision (the weakness is *unbelievable*), and there is always a chance that the hand will begin to recover of its own accord. He believes that it will.

Another decision thrown in my lap. I rise up from the breakfast table the morning I get this letter and start to pace about the room in the most frightful agitation. I go to and fro along the side of the table. What in God's name do I do? If I tell Father, I betray Michael's confidence. And yet doesn't he perhaps want me to do so? Michael has never avoided a decision in his life before, and by letting the matter go out of his hands isn't he indicating that he wants to be taken over? And taken over by Father, who will know the right thing to be done and not make a fuss, not by me, since I'm unsure of the correct course of action and will certainly make a fuss.

As it happens, it's settled for me the same evening when Father comes home. He's wearing a light blue spring suit with a lustrous chocolate-brown Fath tie. His depressions suit him, making him look younger, paler, and tense. He stumbles over a gift-hamper which is lying in the kitchen still unpacked; it arrived a week ago from Fortnum's and contains enough luxuries to feed Michael for the next two months. Frowning and enraged, he says harshly:

'We'd better give it away, if you can't be bothered to unpack it.'

'Well, Father, why don't *you* unpack it?'

He is so surprised at this direct reply, and at the sternness of my tone, that he stops in the middle of mixing a whisky and soda and gets out the tin of indigestion powder. And then, afraid that I may not have noticed what he's doing, he pretends he can't get the lid off.

But the days I've lived through recently, and the sternness of my thoughts, make me invulnerable to his tricks. I say:

'Yes, Father. Indigestion mixture.'

There's at once a change in his attitude. A second later he's drunk the medicine, is looking placidly out of the kitchen window (a thing he would never do ordinarily, the windows of Blenheim or Chambord are the only windows Father could look out of placidly) and even seems to be remaining in the kitchen for the pleasure of my company. Then he gives me a mischievous, comprehending smile, and says:

'By the way, what's this the bank manager tells me about sending money to Karachi? Are you and Michael in business together?'

When he comes to the end of it his eyes are merry. He's overjoyed to think that his two children are up to some commercial dodge and have started to do amusing things on their own account. But if that were true, Father, you know very well you wouldn't be able to get the better of others in business and seduce women, since the things that enable you to do this are my innocence and Michael's integrity. We make you feel guilty, and that's invaluable.

When Father says this I am slicing a large purple beetroot for a salad. I stop fractionally when I hear that I'm discovered, and the icy message goes around my body, and then I get on with my sensuous purple task. But my hands tremble and I'm chilled with discovery and the colder dread of uttering my secret, because I don't think I can find a lie in time, not before looking up, as I must do now, and wiping these red-stained fingers.

With my head still down for safety, I say:

'Michael's ill.'

'Oh. You didn't tell me.'

'No.'

'What is it?'

'Poliomyelitis.'

I can look at him at last, and do so. He usually looks down and away when something is serious, like my one-time Wolf. Without a whiff of accusation he merely asks:

'Is it serious?'

'Yes. I'd better give you the letters.'

I think you had.' For the first time the way he puts it tells me that his attitude towards me has begun to harden.

I bring him the letters with my hands still bloody. They are in date order. He draws a chair up to the davenport in the sitting-room (the one with Michael's photograph on it) and reads them like a boy at a lesson. When he has finished, he looks at me. It's a look I shan't forget. The sort of look that tells you you've never really known someone: it comes from the back of the head where the thoughts are very dark. It tells me that I've lost his love. And he knows now that he lost mine some time ago. Suddenly I learn things about Father like lightning. In ten minutes, or half an hour, everything will be understood and forgiven. Perhaps we shall love each other more, in a new way . . . but I cannot be sure . . . and meanwhile I am growing up.

He says two sentences, accurate, brutal, unforgettable:

'You should have told me about his hand. It may be too late to save it.'

He brings out his diary from a jacket pocket and begins to write something down. I'm turned to stone – the thought that this may be true is enough to lie on my conscience for the rest of my life. Oh but, Father, if only you had been approachable! If only I could have spoken to you normally. But so many fits, so many needs, made you inaccessible. I was your housekeeper-daughter, and must play in my play-pen with my own thoughts and desires and not bother you with them. Can you lock a woman up and load her with tasks and take away her joy, and then expect her confidence? I don't think so.

It occurs to me that he's making plans to fly out to Karachi. And so, with the sharpness of someone not disguising that the underlying thought is sharp, I say:

'You can't go.'

'No. I know that. I'm sending Buffy.'

'Buffy!'

'Yes. He's impersonal.'

'Will he go?'

'Yes. I think so. He may not. But . . . he owes me a good deal. If he can't go, at least he'll contact someone out there.'

Father's going to make Buffy do it for *his sake*. Power again. Fate seems to put all the pawns back into Father's hand. Michael goes all the way to Karachi for the sake of his ideas, and now he's to be brought back, inert, by Buffy, another pawn, and returned to the play-pen where I live. And once there, he'll be written off as a failure, because there's always an idea implicit in people's minds that when a man gets ill it's his own fault, and that he's more or less done it deliberately as a way of getting out of real work, and has probably earned the illness by doing stupid things, living carelessly, not cleaning his teeth . . . and writing poetry. To a materialist, it all adds up and makes for something bad, unwholesome.

I seem to read all this in Father's shoulders. He's writing letters, one to our doctor here, one to the doctor in Karachi, and then . . . one to Michael. He has his hand up over his brow for a long time while thinking this over, and in the end writes just one line. I don't know what it says, but I do know what it costs him. How silently he walks about, putting stamps on the letters himself, not calling out to me to tell him where the stamps are or to fetch them for him. I know he's reproaching himself, and yet I also know that his attitudes are not even dented by the bad news. He makes way for it, as though it was not entirely unexpected. It confirms his belief in the evils of an unbalanced life. He does not sigh deeply, or droop, or needle me, as he has done in every other crisis in life. Just walks about doing things, staring ahead of him and chewing over the facts.

He phones Buffy, and I'm amazed to hear his party voice, relaxed and cheerful, going out over the telephone. The bad news is conveyed almost in an aside, as a slice from a large joint of meat, among slices good, bad, and indifferent, that Father is cutting up at every moment of the day. Going to Karachi is made to seem a perfectly ordinary occurrence for an extremely busy MP but also something that he should have done long ago, and that Father also should have done, in order to inspect some factory developments on which he has been asked to lend money and to meet certain leaders of the one World

Government movement. The fact that Michael is there strengthens the reason for the visit, and he can be of service to Michael, for which Father will be grateful, very grateful indeed. He manages somehow to imply that being paralysed is the end of a continuous party Michael has been at, an inner circle of gaiety, which Buffy too might catch the tail end of if he hurries, since only Michael has the key to this international pleasure-making. Whatever the hold Father has over Buffy, moral or financial, it's effective enough to bring Buffy back to the phone half an hour later to say that he will either go himself as soon as he can clear his diary or see that Michael is contacted in Karachi and brought home by a responsible person. So that's settled. Everything has suddenly become simplified. And within days now Michael will be brought back and will be in the house again. The illness and the suffering are gradually being absorbed into our ordinary life, and are no longer going on in solitude in the desert where I've had them for so long in my mind. My burden is lighter. Speaking of Buffy later in the evening, Father says humorously: 'Anyway, I've got a lot of property in his constituency.' There is a game within every game for him, and this is the way he makes life interesting. When he stops behaving badly, I get on better with my father than I do with anyone else in the world: his devilry is so appealing. But I don't like our relationship, we have this subconscious grudge against one another. I have it because the piece of time I've given to my father was time in which I should have got married and had babies; and then these psychosomatic diseases of his, these inventions which are real, keep me at home pampering him. He has it because now that I've given him a stable domestic life, a rock on which to rebuild his emotions, he feels complete enough to start a new story with a new woman, and I'm in the way. He pays me out for this by teasing me, as a cat does a mouse, by playing on my fear of being expelled and left all alone. It's all subconscious; he knows he has the whip-hand over me, and he knows inwardly that I'm *terrified* – and sometimes he uses it, and sometimes he's magnanimous and doesn't. And meanwhile he is enjoying every single minute of it.

Ah, that's the first time I've thought of anything but Michael's illness for days. I feel I've been disloyal to him by not keeping pace with his solitude and suffering for the last hour as I do normally.

I'm drawing the rose velvet curtains in my bedroom later that night, with both my arms raised, when I'm suddenly reminded of Father's words about Michael's hand. Will it recover? Could I have saved it?

I don't know how to ease my distracted conscience, and stand there murmuring: '*Forgive me.*' I'm moved in turn by the sound of my own voice speaking to itself and the hopelessness of this begging. But it's the only thing to say in life when it's too late and you've failed someone you love.

'Forgive me, oh please forgive me. I didn't realise –'

Thank God Father has taken the essential action, and at once. He understands exactly what to do and how to do it (through Buffy – who doesn't matter) without infuriating Michael. This makes up for everything, and all my silent agonies are worthless by comparison with his kind, decisive measures.

I can hear him passing my room, and I go out and kiss

him impulsively. He holds me and strokes my hair and rocks me slightly. He even soothes me: 'There, there, Pigeon.'

'Oh Father.'

'There, little Pigeon.'

'Did I do wrong?'

'You weren't to know.'

Once again I'm easing my sorrows here against his chest and passing over my conscience to him to have it wiped clean. But didn't Father put it there, on my conscience, so that he could take it away?

He kisses me on my brow, and with the greatest gentleness, looking into my eyes under the electric light and speaking as though it was a natural extension of our previous conversation, he says:

'And you will get rid of that nasty old piano for me, won't you? Because it really is an eyesore, and it's spoiling my music-room.'

11

I am going to see my Wolf again. After such a long interval I can hardly remember what he looks like. When I replied to him, he sent me a fierce, joyful telegram. And then we exchanged letters. I've stopped trying to work out his behaviour, because the twists are incomprehensible. I no longer ask myself whether I want to see him, or do not want to see him. I don't think about his wife. And I don't think about myself. I merely suggest that if he wants to meet me, we have lunch together.

When I was dismissed, I cut my dreaming off in mid-air. I haven't re-started it. I'm so much calmer nowadays; I don't hope or wish for anything too much for myself.

This morning there will be a letter confirming the luncheon appointment and telling me where it is to be. I've begun to sleep so much better these last two days since talking to Father; my own fears seem lightweight, absurd, by comparison with the reality of Michael's condition. Yes, Buffy *is* going, *Buffy* – who won't even talk to the people next to him at a dinner party and is still mentally having tea with Princess Margaret. I'm amazed. But it's true. He leaves this evening. Father has arranged everything, right down to a Rolls to take him to the airport. I'm afraid he understands the chip on Buffy's shoulder much too well.

I'm allowing myself to breakfast late, and in this pretty dressing-gown which goes to the floor rather stiffly like a party-frock. So perhaps, insidiously, I'm not displeased to see this man again. The pockets are stuffed with paper handkerchiefs, and I scrunch them softly as I go down. I'm aware of my hands suddenly and of the way I'm moving . . . already? The morning sunlight falls on to the stair carpet from this east window in a gold oblong, which throws itself down the stairs and keeps the whole flight to the hall at blood heat, like a tiger. I used to sit on these stairs in this same sunshine as a little girl and feel as safe as houses.

Don't worry, my married one, I'm not going to make conditions any more. I shan't press my luck too hard, or ask too much of you. No one will have to make a statement, stand by it, count up to a hundred and hold their breath. I shan't take anything away from you, or hurt your wife; I'll see to it you don't behave badly. I'll keep everything fluid, amusing, uncompromising and gentle.

I go through the letters with indolent fingers. There's the Karachi typewritten envelope: how faithful that good Pakistani friend is. Michael says he comes every day, and they are entirely content in one another's company. Yes, there it is . . . and there's . . . No, an invoice . . . There's . . . No, however much I sort over the letters I cannot find one from my Wolf. It simply isn't there.

Oh not again! I'm not to be hurt again, to have my spirit broken again, for no reason. First that thirty-five minutes at the Ritz, then the famous letter: 'Shall we call the series a draw?' and now . . . nothing, a void, a black hole in the middle of the dining-room, into which I am falling. Not again! No more blocks of suffering to be got through without a sound, like long indigestible meals, before you can get out at the other side. I can hardly count on anything any more. The floor under my feet seems to be giving way. I'm entirely dulled, as though I've been hit on the side of the head with a brick.

It's too much! I fly away to get my writing paper and biro. I bring them back to the breakfast table. I eat what I can eat, and I scribble down a composition, and cross it out and start again. Top off egg and salt carefully into yolk. 'I have just come downstairs and there is no letter from you.' A spoonful of egg, all salt, really. 'You leave me high and dry, not even having the courtesy to clear up a lunch appointment.' Deeply into egg, dark yolk, and swallow down something highly unpleasant attached to it. 'Protecting your own vanity is understood, but what on earth have I done to you –'

I'm saying exactly what I feel. I paint my distress without abuse, which is always a sign of weakness. I don't sign it. He knows my hand. I leave a blank to be filled by my disgust. Then I phone for a cab; there are many worse ways of spending Father's money than paying a cab to carry my protest from Holland Park to the City of London. A whole dark rattling taxi to carry my furious letter – I look in the mirror there in the hall – the letter of a pretty woman who has *had enough*. Since rage, like insomnia, whitens my skin and stretches it more tightly, I look quite pretty this morning And for whom do I look pretty? For *myself*.

I dress, and get about the house. I open windows, scold

the cleaner, make telephone calls. And at eleven o'clock I hear the second post clap through the letter-box and go coldly to pick up the usual nonsensical stuff. And there it is, the letter from my Wolf. There's a fourpenny stamp on it. Oh diabolical post office torture, to give one more turn to the screw. I see from the date stamp that it was posted in London the day before yesterday But after the blow with the brick that I had at breakfast and two hours of broken, disorganised thoughts, I don't *want* this letter. Everything is designed to bring me to the ground and humiliate me. How am I expected to dress and meet a lunch appointment in response to some casual directive that reaches me half-way through the morning? A man with a fourpenny stamp has just lost me for the sake of one penny. I see that he has written on the envelope 'First', meaning it's to be sent by first-class post, but why hand over such a letter to his secretary? Too busy to post it himself? That's hardly likely. No, it was obviously not of the first importance and he did not take trouble over it. Evidently these letters and telegrams are all part of some familiar routine of his, once the appointment has been made, and I've acknowledged that I want to see him, he loses interest again.

I read the letter; it's long and informative, just like the ones we've already exchanged. He went to such and such a party and looked for me, he went to Berlin and saw *Krapp's Last Tape* and bought some china. He missed me all the time. He *missed me* . . . by a penny. We are lunching on anonymous ground, according to him, at the Terrazza. It's a healthy, affectionate letter.

But we are not lunching because I no longer have the strength to go. I could not choose my clothes or do my hair: my hands tremble too much. I have been defeated by these three men in turn, by my father, by Michael, and by fourpenny-stamp Wolf. There will be no lunch and no lover.

The telephone rings. I know instantaneously that it's my Wolf, that he's only just that moment arrived at his office and had my taxi-letter. It's in my mind not to answer, but to turn away from the whole affair. The phone goes on ringing; upbringing and the good habits formed by Father are hard to break, and I go to answer it because it is my duty. And I know as I do that I want to.

'Arabella?' The same light voice! But troubled.

'Yes . . . it's all right. I got it. Second post.' How fast I can speak.

'Oh thank God for that.' Emotion and open relief.

There's a second between us. He says:

'Can I come round this afternoon?'

'What time?'

'Two o'clock?'

'All right.'

'All right. See you then.'

It takes one minute to make an appointment for which we've both waited two months. I've made concessions and, worse, admissions. Toppled out of my haughty, upright posture by a man who gets his own way by ravaging my thoughts, I've been caught by the telephone at a moment of indecision. We had begun to get to know one another by letter, and after opening my mind to his thoughts I hadn't yet been able to close it swiftly enough. I should have slammed it shut and been free of him. Instead, I'm more disturbed, more caught than ever. My fatal mistake is to stay at home and think, because it's by my thoughts that this Wolf has caught me.

At two o'clock. The clock seems to be jumping forward, ten minutes at a time. And I can't plan, just when I need absolute self-possession. Events have fallen *his* way; he has an appointment with me at home, a thing he's always wanted.

I must do everything to protect myself. I must be a bitch, I owe it to myself. The people who are about in the world today don't have feelings that in any way resemble mine; it's a form of idiocy, which is out of date. I must learn to be casual and learn fast . . . by two o'clock.

What shall I wear? I go through my entire wardrobe cupboard. No, no, no, a dress is so – provincial, a trouser-suit so – nautical. None of these colours suit me. I drag all my sweaters and blouses out and turn them over. I must wear something which is always lucky for me and which has no memories about it. It's no good, I can't visualise myself today, I'm too nervous. Suppose I stay as I am? Pulling clothes over my head always makes me pale and fretful. I'm wearing a porridge-coloured string sweater with a knitted collar open at the neck, brown velvet trousers and gold chain – at one moment it's too hot, and at the next I add to it a long brown velvet cardigan that goes to my knees, because I'm cold, freezing cold with stage fright.

And I must have something to do when he arrives. Because to have empty hands and to seem to be waiting for him will only feed this spoilt over-nourished Wolf. I must have something to do, since then I can look at it, for I can't look at him, already the thought of having to look at him is terrible.

I quickly assemble some tasks in the sitting-room. I can't write to Michael, because my letter won't get there in time, but I'll read through today's letter – for the fiftieth time, because although I've been reading it since nine o'clock, I don't know what it says. (Was it only last night that I faltered in my bedroom, and uttered the words 'Forgive me'?) And now I don't care, and shall pretend to do some sewing of course, sewing on my mother's sewing machine, to deceive a man. I lift it to the strong little table and remove the curved lid like that of a toy cathedral. I begin to prepare a spool with purple cotton.

Who will let him in? The cleaner has gone and I'm alone. I haven't the strength to go to the door; besides, front-door confrontations belong to the whole street, they're ignominious . . . the white daylight pours in, we stand facing one another like two butlers . . . unthinkable. I rush to the hall and quickly open the door and stick the front-door key into it. He can let himself in . . . I shall be sewing, coldly, bitchily, as in a Dutch interior. Suppose he doesn't see the key? I rush to Father's desk and, taking a white sheet of paper, I jab the key through it and then into the lock. There; it has a great white pie-frill around it like a leg of mutton. Wolf, Wolf, I hope you're worthy of me.

I return to the sitting-room in a state of extreme tension. It's just gone one-twenty; I find I can't focus very well. Threading the needle of the sewing-machine means bending down sideways, and in the warm, light-coloured sitting-room – it's like the stairs this morning, pale, alive (nearly breathing), like a well-kept body – I keep licking the cotton and pointing it sideways, while my mind, in which variegated thoughts are swirling around at such a rapid speed, prevents me again and again from getting it into the eye of the needle.

I hear rapid steps up to the front door. How early! But I was expecting him. The key is turned in an instant, and the door opens. He's in the house!

Not a word. He doesn't call out. I hear him put down something – a despatch case? He enters the sitting-room, looking for me. He's seen me, and comes over. I dare not look up, I'm so full of dread; it's impossible. He goes down on one knee beside me, and I'm lifted against his chest and have my head continuously held and kissed. I can't tell whether I'm sitting, still, or am in the process of falling to the floor. I have no thoughts; they've left me. I vaguely make out a shirt-front, blue tie, the lower half of a dark jaw with a serious, unsmiling mouth set into it. I'm held for a long time. I recover slightly, almost enough to speak. What has happened? I'm bound against another human being; I can't move away; I'm lost. There is a form of tranquil energy in this man which has the effect of taking away all my thoughts, my ability to move, even desire itself. It is lulling, supernatural, positive, and while I am able to drink it with my thirsty body I am perfectly contented.

He wants to kiss me, and moves me a little to do so. For the first time in my life, I'm the one who gets tired, who faints with the dead-weight of lust in the middle of a kiss, and have to have my mouth held tenderly in his, until I have the strength to pick it up and go back to the silent, tiring centre of the work.

No, we can't kiss for long. We're too tired, too care-worn by waiting and by misunderstandings. It's much more important to hold one another and to get closer and to try to repair ourselves in this glowing bath of electricity we've made for one another . . . until we're well enough to speak, and then it won't matter what we say in any case. Everything has been understood: I am not a bitch, and he is not a wolf. And our present occupation is the most serious in the world.

We re-adjust ourselves. I find that I am on the floor; I must have slipped down when my sinews melted, and here I am, sitting comfortably on my heels as only dancers or young children can. He is still on one knee, it forms a right angle as firm as iron, and is a chairback for me, against which I lean to have my mouth stroked by his, or by his cheeks, or his brow, or the side of his head, as thick as a cropped-down forest, that smells of shampoo. My arms go around him and hold the cloth of his jacket, because I know he wants to be held, and then they drop away when my strength leaves me.

So this long embrace, obtained at the eleventh hour, goes on and on in the sitting-room, and is all the work of a fourpenny stamp. I've landed in these arms when I should, by rights, be winding up a luncheon, controlled, witty, and self-contained. Time and our thoughts have piled up and up, and flung us against one another so that we cannot separate – not until ordinary life wears its way through to us again.

By degrees I feel well enough and courageous enough to look at him without fainting, and do so quickly when there is an opportunity between the amorous movements of his head. He does not look at me, he's too intelligent for such a blunder, but concentrates on me as though using his whole body to see me. There is enough power left over for us to be ourselves, within the embrace, and to pick up or put down the love-making when we want to, without forcing our personalities, and to find ourselves gradually.

I am about to speak, and he says in a low, wise voice, overcome by emotion:

'Don't talk, Arabella.'

I won't talk, my Wolf, so long as I am understood.

Presently we want to get up; and he helps me to my feet. We walk a little together, not really knowing whether we are walking or still down on the floor. A few steps along the room and we are opposite the little chaise where Father sat and waited for me that evening I was late. This man is so intuitive that this thought of mine stops him, and he turns to me. It's almost as though he's teaching Father a lesson by acting for him, beside the couch where he sat so ill-humouredly, the gravity and depth of our passion.

And he places his right hand around my neck, which is bent back, and I reach up my left hand and run it freely over the beautiful head and down the neck. And we take our second kiss, standing, soaked in one another, and satisfying one another level by level, because we have begun to think. And there is more sex and less ecstasy in it, and the sex is not innocent. It is the serious sex that makes you cry.

Then I find out that I can't stand any longer, since I'm worn out. We collapse onto the sofa, and the thread is broken. We can see one another, and we begin to smile, and we're friends.

He tells me how wretched he's been: 'I was even sharp to waiters.' I ask him:

'But why did you shoot me down?'

'Because you said you weren't going to see me again.'

'But that was malicious, to get a letter in first like that.'

'Well, I thought that if I suggested quickly in a letter that we saw each other only now and again, you wouldn't cut me out altogether.'

'Oh. I thought it was a piece of condescending kindness from someone who was moving on around the mad-hatter's tea-party and was already two beds away.'

He shakes his head, smiling. And he looks straight at me – for the first time! Even so I catch his thought and reprove him:

'And don't start that "will you come and sleep with me?" routine, for God's sake.'

'I won't. It doesn't mean I don't want to. But it doesn't any longer seem to be of primary importance.'

'Oh Jesus, you're attacking from a new angle.'

'No, I'm not. You must believe me.'

I say unfairly:

'Then you're not normal.'

We wait while this passes away. We're very happy, and look one another over with gratified glances, very secure and exhilarated. We tell one another everything. I speak of Michael. He's concerned; anything that affects me affects him. He asks to see today's letter. I'm so astonished that I should be of importance to anyone that I can't believe he's serious. And so at first I refuse to bring it. Later I bring it to him, and read it again for the fifty-first time, resting inside his arm which encloses me with a new love I have never felt before.

(And throughout all these events, even when I was partially unconscious in the middle of a kiss, because we are so happy and right for one another I have been deciding that I must give him up. And the reason is that it's serious.)

We read the letter together, as though we do this habitually. The complete change of attitude since that first dinner with a hostile, contradictory stranger is so extraordinary that I continually look up at him bewildered with wide-open eyes and he, each time, kisses my nose as though he has never done anything else. And goes on reading, and even makes out Michael's new shuddering script: '*The old fan-blade dried my sickbed/With antique rotations.*' It's the first two lines of a poem he's writing.

Oh Michael, I forgot you. For a whole hour. Or is it two?

My Wolf says:

'I'd like to meet him.'

'I'd like you to. But – I've sold him down the line to Buffy and Father.'

'To save his hand.'

'He won't forgive me. Michael never sells out. You'll see. He'll say I've betrayed him to the idiots.'

'He was leaning on you too heavily.' He lifts me thoughtfully on to his lap, and tucks me in towards him so that his head can rest itself in my neck and I can barber this curly hair of his with my mouth and with both my hands, which at once go over it looking for trouble. His ears are small and I go over the upper rim of the one I'm offered in the way we used to test the edge of a jam tart in the nursery. He blows softly into the cut of my string jersey, and says:

'You never sold anyone down the line in your life, Arabella.'

I'm horrified, he's an *idealist*! If he goes on like this I shall lose my bitchiness, the only thing I have left. He's been building up an image all this time; he's building the sort of woman he wants. It's not myself at all. I'm an insecure luxury object, a boudoir cat, spoilt – as spoilt as he is – horribly nervous, rather grasping of material possessions, accustomed to giving orders to one set of human beings and receiving them from another set – from Father and from Michael. I say in jerks:

'You don't know anything about it. I'm selling you down the line right now.' What I mean is that he is giving me love; I can feel it and I am afraid, and want to back away.

'And I'm enjoying every minute of it,' he says happily.

He wants me to wind my way into his heart, and he makes sure that all my remarks show my good-nature, or disguise it, so that only *he* can see through the device.

There's so much sunlight in the room, I keep blinking. A man goes by in the street outside singing loudly and in tune. Everything confirms my Wolf in his high opinion of me; I even seem to be able to control the weather, and to change this district of London into a carefree Latin Quarter where promenading people sing out loud for joy.

He's convinced that nothing can spoil our rapture, and talks on freely, asking me in future to trust him absolutely and to confide in him. (But won't there then be two of us trusting him, his wife and myself?) Even so, mentally, these are so much words that I long to hear that I'm wooed by them, and my soul stretches at every minute and grows, since it's always ready nowadays to seize on those things which will help it to grow so that it's strong enough to leave home and Father. In between this verbal love-making, or rather soul-making, are slashed in quick pictures, spontaneous carnal photographs, of our eventual meeting in bed. They knock the breath out of me.

In extreme danger, and sinking, metaphorically I put my hand out for dry land . . . something with hard edges . . . money? Everything depends on not being a baby at this moment in life. I feel grateful to the cast of mind I have inherited from Father, when it supplies me, in my hour of need, with a fourpenny stamp. My thoughts come to a halt. I ask with deceitful dreaminess:

'Why didn't you post the letter yourself?'

He stops the lullaby he's been making with his breath and kisses, almost stops breathing, and replies as openly as anyone can when they are walking across an open fire on bare feet:

'As a rule I always post letters to you myself. But it happened last Wednesday that I had to rush to a meeting at five and couldn't get to the post myself. I didn't want to miss it, so I wrote "First" on the letter and gave it to my secretary. I couldn't know that she would only put a fourpenny stamp on it. And even with a fourpenny stamp, it should have arrived by first post today. But I'm glad it didn't.'

That final sentence is so smug that it makes me jump to attention. I snap:

'I don't retract what I wrote.'

My Wolf lifts up his head, and looks at me solemnly as though I've shouted in a church service.

'Hush,' he says.

When I send him away after tea, there's a seal on our

relationship the size of the Magna Carta seals. We've both put our hands to it and signed, in our own blood, once or twice for fun with flourishes, and all the time irredeemably in pledges that live off the page. The bed has been spoken for via the heart. The only question then is: shall I be able to give him up afterwards? But if we make love, at least it will take away the edge of his desire, and so preserve him for his wife.

And this time it's my own life – not a play, or an opera – that is passing down my spine a draughty breath, cold enough to make my flesh creep. It doesn't feel like pleasure, so it must be fate.

12

The very last letter from Karachi.

Michael's bed has been made up in his old room on the second floor, everything is ready if he should come today, or tomorrow, or the next day.

The part of the letter in Michael's spider crawl goes: 'I haven't decided yet whether I shall come. I do not want to put myself back in that man's power.' 'That man' is, of course, Father.

Michael says nothing about my betrayal; I suppose that from now on I am one of *'Them'*, the Judas Iscariots who betray with love, or just a ruthless Miss Mouse. He simply won't bother to talk openly to me ever again; that's how it will be. My wildness wasn't the equal of his. If this last manuscript letter of his, half type, half scribble, could utter some sound that conveyed the journey of his thoughts from the sickbed across land and water to me, it would be a low, piteous, howling noise. The permanent loss of his hand is really nothing to him; it's a bore, that's all. He lives in his mind, and India is filled with broken human bodies – it's the custom there to be broken, or to seek it – and men who live in their minds. It's we, Father and I, who can't bear the thought of that hand. It hurts us to think about it, and our desire to recover it is very largely selfish.

I know that he will return, because the longing to put feet on English ground will be too strong. You do not refuse Paradise. And especially when you have been a god there.

The details of a sick man's daily life in Pakistan are as gritty, rusty, as that hook on Michael's window which has gone on squeaking all these days, all that afternoon while I kissed my Wolf. The same hot, wet breeze has been twitching it. And the English sun, the sitting-room sun we used as a pleasant yellow bath for ourselves, is there a monstrosity in the sky, something in flames, unbelievable, giving a light in which there is no object as far as the horizon you can touch without burning yourself.

Since he can go neither upstairs nor downstairs unaided, but can only drag himself along on a level, Abdul carries him up to the flat roof every evening, and there he goes round and round on a piece of featureless concrete, staring over the parapet at monotonous rubble desert where nothing grows. He has begun to fall; apparently this is a hazard with paralytics. If there is a little abrasion in the concrete and his sandal catches it, he falls full length, unable to save himself. 'Like a man in an opera,' writes Michael. He has fallen once on his brow and passed out.

This caged promenade every evening as the sun goes down is the high spot of his day. It's boring, he says, in the way that most physical occurrences, except love-making, are boring. Slices of red life left over by the sun go on lying, smoking hot, on the horizon for half an hour after it has gone.

For the rest he says that the doctor has invented some imbecile exercises in an effort to detect life in his right hand and arm. He is to try to move his hand on a tray of talcum powder, and to roll a ping-pong ball there, so that any movement is written in the white powder. Not content with this, he says, they tell him that he must make a mental effort to *imagine* the movement in advance, and it's this which is so tiring. Now that his hand is free of the plaster cast, the doctor has constructed from leather a species of glove, which, he says, will hold the fingers in the position they should take up in normal functioning, but from which they have fallen into an unnatural heap.

His nurse succeeded at last in getting him into a bath. It was a disaster. When she had filled the bath a third with warm water (Michael says it was *boiling*) she helped him in, and his weak leg promptly collapsed and he fell nearly under the water, being unable to use his arms at all. He was in such a state of terror that he implored her to call his bearer and to lift him out straight away. Whereupon she was affronted in her professional vanity, and refused, and continued to wash him while holding his head above the water. Michael said his life hung by the thread of her goodwill, and he knows now how babies must feel when they are bathed. He bore with it, looking up at her with his eyes smarting with tears, and having to pretend, as children often have to, that it was a good idea and that he was even enjoying it. Michael says she robbed him of his dignity and he has hated her ever since. Those are the only tears he has shed throughout, and his pride bleeds to remember them.

On most days he wears a khaki shirt, tied around the middle with string, and pyjama trousers.

He is taken in to the Seventh Day Adventist hospital by taxi across the desert every three days, and on the first occasion, after they had set three strong nurses on him, they decided to treat him with hot saline blankets. Michael says this is known as the Sister Kenny treatment, and he recommends it to all embryo torturers. The blankets – which were thick dark brown wool – were taken from a steaming hot cupboard. They themselves were at a temperature close to boiling point. In the unbearable midday heat (117°) they were wrapped around his naked body until he thought he would faint away altogether. They were then removed and he was placed under an iced-cold shower. He was then left to rest, in a shocked condition. He had no idea what the next instalment of treatment was likely to be, but lay there desperately inventing measures to protect himself. He was subsequently wheeled into a room to be massaaged with olive oil by a large pleasant American with rather dirty hands, who was in charge of the hospital gardens. During the massage there was some religious conversation and he was told that the staff at the hospital prayed for him. He asked them to stop this *at once*, because, he said, 'it stank'. 'I told them I wasn't a frosted Christian brought up on Ludo.'

He was then wheeled under an ultraviolet lamp which was operated by a friendly, haphazard woman who wore no protective glasses, nor gave him any. With this one eye still half-obscured by its lid, and the other subject to these muscular fixes of which he has written before, he was again terrified of having his sight damaged even further. He got her to promise that the lamp should only be left on for the minimum period of two minutes and that the mouth of the lamp was kept well away from his face. He closed his eyes and repeated a poem by Heine, '*Die arme Seele spricht zum Leibe*', and then shouted for it to be turned off. It was; and a few days later the skin began to peel off his burnt stomach and thighs, which are now excessively tender.

Michael writes that I can imagine that the last few ounces of flesh he had on him have rapidly disappeared since he attended the hospital. He says it is a skeleton who writes to me, soaked with fever, but that he is mentally at perfect peace, and talks every day to Ahmed Choudhri, a poet, who is typing this letter for him.

He says the final absurdity is a recurrence of his early foot trouble. In his poor state of health the wound made by the nail in the flesh of the toe has suppurated, and he has the beginnings of a gangrenous condition. This is interesting because gangrene is *alive*, and does not give you any rest, but fizzes and spits out sparks like a slow-burning firework, especially a slow Catherine wheel. They are going to operate on it, and then the foot must be kept up to drain the wound.

He does not say that he is looking forward to coming home, and he does not send me his love. I know that he will rend me with a fit of silence. It's more bearable somehow now that I've signed this temporary lovers' Magna Carta with my Wolf. I know quite well that I've betrayed Michael first and foremost for my own peace of mind. You must not love your brother too much; and it is forbidden to be in love with him. And after all what could I give him in the end? Not myself. It occurs to me that it's only I myself who think that Michael is unhappy. He doesn't think so. His state of mind is the only thing he cares about, and that's the very thing I've endangered by putting him back into Father's power. I suppose I was always trying to give him a life he didn't want, together with amusements, objects, ideas and attitudes he didn't want, and the sort of happiness which to him would be unhappiness. But from my point of view his life is an open wound.

All these letters from him are the letters of an arrogant boy whose spirit is unbroken and whose heart *hasn't even started to beat*. I know that, because mine has started . . . from the afternoon when I was trying to run some purple thread through the sewing machine and my Wolf made me so intolerably, agonisingly happy, against my will, by teaching me to love him. Quite unfair. It begins the day you stop loving *things* and start loving people.

Another point about these letters is that Michael, lying in his khaki shirt tied with string, never for a moment stops patronising Father, directly or by implication. As though he has somehow achieved something by climbing on a sickbed and getting paralysed, by the mere process of gaining a new point of view. He quotes humorously from the poem he's writing: '*That terrible anguish I though would crush me / Has, in fact, crushed me.*'

With both Michael and Father, each one thinks he is in charge of the relationship, and that power over other is invested in him.

This last letter ends with a reference to obtaining some clothes, a light tropical suit which will disguise his condition, and also crutches. So I know very well that he *will* return with Buffy. He says that from now on he is separated forever from the English poets by his sufferings and his experience, whereas before he was separated only by his contempt.

Now that we expect him any day, there's a different feeling about in the house. Imperceptibly our behaviour is changing. Father laughs more often. The day before yesterday I saw him frowning at a rather vulgar bright blue porcelain bowl in the sitting-room; today I notice it's gone. So has the photograph of Michael from the desk; very wise, Father. And then yesterday evening Father walked in wearing an entirely new kind of tie – with too much fruit salad, too much of the gutter in it – and a brown leather waistcoat straight out of the King's Road. I couldn't take my eyes off it. I've never seen him in anything but city suits or tweeds before, and now the centre of his body has the appearance of a boa-constrictor, supple, implacable, shiny, new, fond of swallowing things whole and taking ultraviolet sunbaths.

Since we found one another out – over Michael – and for a while lost one another's love, we've been a great deal more light-hearted together. It seems to have lifted a weight from our relationship; the heavy, angry, dependent love has gone, and the soaking-wet sentiment which belonged to the past. We were living our life together too thoroughly, and now we can skimp a bit.

Father runs upstairs lightly (stopping to straighten a crooked picture which could irritate Michael if he were to arrive today) because he knows now he hasn't got me around his neck for the rest of his life. He's found out that I think my own thoughts and act on them. He even nags me in a new way, and I know that this nagging of his is part of his way of loving someone.

What *is* it that Michael is bringing us that we have been doing without? A way of making life young and amusing. Michael used to have a list, a menu of the street corners in Europe where you could stand about and live a twenty-four-carat life, getting a shallow, casual, diamond joy that could last you for the rest of your days. Once you have this infection, I believe it can't be cured. When there's too much mauve in a face, from the streets, you can't get it out again. The racing and gambling set were all right according to Michael, but they still had a touch of the potato about them, they were organised entertainments, not haphazard dangers like those laid on by life.

Michael's way of dealing with life is to be outside it, just as Father's is to be deep inside it. And then Michael has this sense of a destiny he must fulfil; this is what used to irritate poor Father so much, because he was just *living*, like everyone else.

But there have been moments in the last few days – what with so much changing of sides – when we all three, yes and my Wolf, making four, seemed to be on the same side! Father, Michael, myself, and Wolf. I don't know what moral trick we played on one another, unless it was idealism in four different forms.

And my Wolf, what about him? This hot fire that I go to mentally with my head bent and my eyes, with tears in them, kept down – I won't force it, and I won't seek it; but I shall no longer refuse the body that kisses first like a boy, and then like nobody on earth. Even so I murmur: 'Don't give me love' because I know that love-making depends on the spirit in which it is done, and so – I'm very much afraid.

There's the key. It's Father, home on the dot. He's looking very pleased with himself, and can hardly contain the good cheer he's picked up from somewhere. There's a trace of shyness, a rod down the centre of his body, and he's carrying an object, very small and square, protectively bandaged over and over with new, white tissue paper. It's the size of a snuff-box and he gives it into my hands and looks at me with joyful, light-filled eyes.

'What is it, Father?'

'A present. For Pigeon.'

He kisses me all over my brow, not caring whether he hits skin or hair or how messily he does it – just like a lion-like country dog with a gentle nature.

I unwrap it, while he watches darkly, proudly . . . and there's a familiar little leather box . . . and inside, click . . . there's my dear old Cabochon ruby ring! Father's traced it and bought it back for me; he's forgiven me and loves me. I'm overwhelmed, and deeply, timidly happy to be loved again. My own feels like cupboard love by comparison.

'You must put it on,' says Father, giving orders at once.

'Yes, of course.'

I slip on this great piece of raspberry sugar and twizzle it slightly on my finger so that Father can get the full feminine value of the sugary stone swirled about on a white finger, just above the knuckle. I say:

'She doesn't flash, she broods; she's an electric fire.'

Father is pleased that I've appreciated the nature of the stone. He watches me playing with it for a while, and then suddenly sheers off into the kitchen. A few minutes later I hear chopping noises, very methodical and regular. Good Lord, I haven't heard that domestic sound for some months now, and I know instantly what it is. Father is making one of his soups. Just in time for Michael's arrival!

But . . . instinct tells me to fly.

I must get away; quickly. Before they close in on me again, with soup and poetry. I find I don't want to lend Michael my brain any more, so that he can expand and store his ideas in it. I don't want to be a credit to Father. I don't want to be trapped in a sitting-room and taught to love a married Wolf. I do . . . and I don't. I tell myself: 'Put the situation into financial terms, you can cure any false magic that way. Is my Wolf prepared to take me on financially in any way? Why couldn't I have gone to *him* to borrow money for Michael? You see? He'll give me everything – in words. But isn't that the sheep's clothing on the Wolf? Don't start enjoying life casually again on *their* terms. Look hard at the facts which underlie your daily life; they're wrong.'

Now that I've thought of it, I see that it's the solution. I must go while I still have this strength. I've found out that strength is silent; it doesn't have to be talked about, proved, or borrowed from others. It isn't even called strength, but action. I've been living as though life went on forever and there was time for everything; but it doesn't. I shall stay on exactly one month to settle Michael in, and that will be the end.

Oh – the smell of that soup from the kitchen. I've just got it in my nostrils, and it's gassing me; I can't breathe. ('If you want to know what's driving me out, it's the gluey pots in the kitchen.') But the stone on my finger is heavy and still cold from the shop.

In the morning the front-door bell rings continuously.

First a telegram to say that Michael arrives this afternoon, and immediately afterwards a messenger carrying red roses in cellophane paper. I behave as though I've never had flowers sent to me before, and take them into the very centre of the sitting-room like a barbarian. I kneel down on the carpet and unwrap them, possessing first the new slippery cellophane, then the white backing paper and silver-paper vase scrunched around the stalks by a flower-shop hand. I look everywhere for a message; there isn't one. Then I count them very carefully; twelve. For one bad moment I thought there were thirteen. I lift them close to my face to get the essence, and the petals feel very like flesh, alive, not so different from the skin of my Wolf, whose presence I can feel here with me so strongly. Even so I have a moment of doubt; ever since that dismissal letter I've been alert for further goodbye surgery; could it be that it's his polite way of signing off again? Not to send a message, presupposing that everything is understood between us, is elegant – but my old doubt is awake and stirring. And even if the roses mean that I am loved, then that reinforces my reason for leaving. The more I am loved, the more I must go. I bolt this thought in behind all my other thoughts. The more Father brings me rings, the more I must go, in case I am bought again with love and money. One more month, and that will be the last.

The fact is that just recently I've been finding Father very irritating. When the air clears and the orders stop raining down on my head, I can see quite clearly for myself that the reason he's so bad-tempered is that fundamentally he's an extremely lazy man; he never does anything for himself, but only tells you how to do it, and is rude to you into the bargain. He calls this 'a genius for organisation'. But putting your finger on other people's weaknesses isn't so difficult, especially when you know your own as well as Father does. He tends therefore to raise himself up by undermining the self-confidence of others, and there must be better ways. Poor Father; what he is really doing is nagging himself and being rude to himself.

Only Michael is a match for him, especially since each thinks he's winning! Father wants Michael here because Michael doesn't want to be here. And if Father has a bad conscience because his son won't even tell him when he's ill, why, he shovels it on my shoulders and I carry the guilt for that hand.

I bang the stalks of the roses with the rounded bone handle of the bread-knife in the kitchen, to open them. Then I give them a long quart vase of water to drink in. I carry them upstairs, not, as I might once have done, to Michael's room, to make it even more beautiful, but to my own. To my own room for the first time in my life I take this love which (temporarily) has been given to me.

Father's sister, Zoë, arrives, out of the blue and all dressed up, hoping to see Michael.

'Is he here?' She looks for the 'remains' like a vulture.

'No. Hasn't arrived yet.'

'But you've got his room ready I hope?' She really is inquisitorial.

'Yes. I've got his room ready.' How weary my voice is. I suddenly say calmly: 'But I can't look after him hand and foot, I've got my own life to lead.' This is so much the opposite of my anxious, compassionate thinking that I don't know how I managed to get it out of the same head which is thinking such different thoughts. A triumph.

'Of course you have. He needs a trained nurse. I shall tell your father so.'

She thoroughly approves of my sensible attitude. In her black-gloved fingers she's carrying a tiny marbled book with rich leather spine and gold tooling on it. The print inside must be minute, almost unreadable. But it's Zoë's idea of a book, and she's brought it especially for Michael.

'I brought this *Purgatorio* in Italian for Michael. I do hope he'll read it.'

'It's very pretty.'

'An illness can be a really valuable time to catch up with your reading. Has Michael still got that frightful Cézanne in his room, the one with the great big bodies? Of course he was no draughtsman, everybody knew that, none of them have got any feet. You know, it's just as decadent as stiletto heels and off-the-shoulder dresses, when you come down to it.'

She's obviously in a frenzy to spring-clean Michael's soul, which got him into all this trouble in the first place. She wants to start him off all over again with good habits, and thinks we should sneak upstairs and make off with the tainted pictures before it's too late. I don't know what that crack about stiletto heels means; she used to wear them herself at one time.

'Michael isn't mad about hands and feet at the moment.'

'Oh no . . . of course not.' She squeezes her nose in a bunch of lace, upset.

As I walk her to the front door, she asks in an intimate voice:

'Have you ordered the wheel-chair?'

I can't answer her. I can literally feel from inside my mouth the same almost brutal shape I've often seen forming on Father's. I know now what causes it: extreme distaste.

Zoë says:

'I'll always come round and push him, you know. Any afternoon.'

She goes off, well satisfied, almost licking her lips.

Michael will be here soon after five o'clock. I'm alone in the house, waiting. Father has again arranged a Rolls with a driver, to please Buffy. Buttering both sides of the bread like that is going to make it even easier for Buffy to pick out books written by Durham miners' sons. Father's too shrewd to go to the airport himself, and he doubts very much whether I can find it in my car which always breaks down when it has to go to boring places.

It's a perfect London afternoon. Sunny, cool streets where you can hear every footfall sharply.

I'm at the curved window, can't help it (it's like standing at the bottom of a decanter), and keep looking down the road.

I see them coming – at last! Here's the big black enamel cabinet bringing Michael. I can't see into the back; too much smog inside. But the driver is one of those omelette-faced men, deadpan, in a peaked cap, a dummy who drives, without moving a muscle, from somewhere far down his body. The tyres munch up some gravel, and the whole thing rests. It's all so English. Somewhere inside is a grey, angry Michael. I wonder if Buffy will try to help him out; he's sure to, with all that stupefying red hair to make it even more ignominious. He'll caper about like an overgrown dancing doll.

I'm keyed up to a pitch of tension when a long pause makes my nerves tingle. I dare not go out, because for Michael to be watched at such a moment, and to have to put on a show, would be hideous.

The dummy driver is first out. He runs around the car, opens the other front door, and with expert movements takes out a pair of aluminium crutches. How they love an illness, a real illness that you can see, and especially a well-paid-up illness with fitments.

He opens the back door of the car tenderly, and a Bob Dylan song swims out from the interior ... '*Stay, lady, stay; stay with your man a while.*'

He then takes a crutch in either hand and lodges them in the gravel on either side of the opening. But instead of bending to the interior and making some motion of assistance he stands well back. A moment later a right foot, together with tropical trouser-leg of manila colour, is stuck out of the car, and it gives the right-hand crutch a sharp kick that puts it into a flowerbed ... Oh yes, I know that egocentric foot ...

VINTAGE CLASSICS

Vintage launched in the United Kingdom in 1990, and was originally the paperback home for the Random House Group's literary authors. Now, Vintage comprises some of London's oldest and most prestigious literary houses, including Chatto & Windus (1855), Hogarth (1917), Jonathan Cape (1921) and Secker & Warburg (1935), alongside the newer or relaunched hardback and paperback imprints: The Bodley Head, Harvill Secker, Yellow Jersey, Square Peg, Vintage Paperbacks and Vintage Classics.

From Angela Carter, Graham Greene and Aldous Huxley to Toni Morrison, Haruki Murakami and Virginia Woolf, Vintage Classics is renowned for publishing some of the greatest writers and thinkers from around the world and across the ages – all complemented by our beautiful, stylish approach to design. Vintage Classics' authors have won many of the world's most revered literary prizes, including the Nobel, the Booker, the Prix Goncourt and the Pulitzer, and through their writing they continue to capture imaginations, inspire new perspectives and incite curiosity.

In 2007 Vintage Classics introduced its distinctive red spine design, and in 2012 Vintage Children's Classics was launched to include the much-loved authors of our childhood. Random House joined forces with the Penguin Group in 2013 to become Penguin Random House, making it the largest trade publisher in the United Kingdom.

@vintagebooks